HOPES AND DREAMS

Other books by Rob Frost:

Methods of Mission (Methodist Publishing House, 1979)

Big Questions (Bible Society, 1983)

Conversation Starters (Bible Society, 1983)

Break Me, Shape Me (Marshall Pickering, 1986)

Go for Growth (Bible Society, 1986)

Visions (Bible Society, 1986)

Breaking Bread (Kingsway, 1988)

People at Work (Pergamon Educational Productions, 1988)

Pilgrims (Kingsway, 1990)

Gospel End (Monarch, 1991)

Broken Cross (Monarch, 1992)

Burning Questions (Monarch, 1994)

When I Can't Pray (Kingsway, 1995)

Thinking Clearly About God and Science (with David Wilkinson) (Monarch, 1996)

For Such a Time as This (Scripture Union, 1996)

Which Way for the Church? (Kingsway, 1997)

A New Start (with David Wilkinson) (Hodder & Stoughton, 1999)

HOPES
AND DREAMS

A Novel by

ROB FROST

MONARCH
BOOKS

Copyright © Rob Frost 1999
The right of Rob Frost to be identified as
author of this work has been asserted by him in
accordance with the Copyright, Designs
and Patents Act 1988

First published by Monarch Books 1999

ISBN 1 85424 426 4

Editorial office: Monarch Books,
Broadway House, The Broadway, Crowborough,
East Sussex TN6 1HQ

Unless otherwise stated, Scripture quotations are
taken from the Holy Bible, New International Version,
© 1973, 1978, 1984 by the International Bible Society.
Used by permission of Hodder and Stoughton Ltd.
All rights reserved.

British Library Cataloguing Data
A catalogue record for this book is available
from the British Library.

Designed and produced for the publisher by
Bookprint Creative Services
PO Box 827, BN21 3YJ, England.
Printed in Great Britain.

Contents

ACKNOWLEDGEMENTS

Thanks to everyone who hosted me during my sabbatical in the summer of 1998 during the writing of this novel:

Perry and Ann Dalton in Pensacola, USA
Clifford and Doris Jenkins in Mumbles, Wales
Malcolm and Janet McCall in Shetland
David and Ann Brown in the *Tees Bruin* Narrowboat
Mike and Cheryl Frith in Kampala
Dr Paul and Dr Rachel Lindoewood at Maua
    Methodist Hospital, Kenya
Ray Dawson at Elm House Centre in Leyburn.

And thanks to all who helped with reading and making suggestions: Michael Whelton, Richard and Meryl Smith, Roland Bryan, Fi McCurdy, Andrew Frost, Jacqui Frost, Clive and Jane Tarrant. Most of all, thanks to Tony Collins, a publisher who really cares about his books.

Prologue

31 December AD 499. 11 pm: Worm's Head

It was dark and very cold. Maidoc was seated cross-legged just inside the opening to his cave. He pulled the hood of his thick woollen habit over his head and gathered it tight under his thick full beard. His bright blue eyes shone out from the hood, they were stinging with the cold.

He was looking out at the dark night beyond. The wind was blowing the rough coarse grass outside, and in the distance he could hear that the surf was up. The wind howled along the ridge of the cliff, its eerie moan accentuating his sense of isolation.

Maidoc was a Celtic hermit, and like the desert fathers in Egypt from whom he gained his inspiration, he was a wise counsellor, occasional miracle-worker and apocalyptic prophet of the Most High God. He was also a man. A very ordinary man. A man who was battling with the demons of his failure and his past.

Maidoc lived in one of the most wild and remote places in Wales, a rocky outcrop known for centuries as 'The Worm'. He had just consumed the last remaining portion of the laverbread which was his supper. He had gathered the thin sheets of seaweed the previous day. These membranes of laver were plastered lankly over the low rocks and stones on the east of Middle Worm.

Laver was mostly a blackish-brown colour, but

further up the shore the young plants were dark red and the fronds long and shredded. He had boiled the pot of laver over his fire for several hours, and gradually the seaweed had been transformed into a sticky black dish which looked unappetising but which tasted delicious. Sometimes those who made the pilgrimage to see Maidoc on Middle Worm brought food with them to share, but, especially in the stormy weather of December, he often had to feed himself by his own ingenuity.

As a young man he had belonged to a close-knit family. He had known the pleasure of a woman's company, and he had once been married. He had savoured the wonder of true love, the joy of good food and strong ale, and the safe laughter of old friends.

And now? People looked on him as some kind of holy man. A great wise sage. A man who talked with God. But he was still the same underneath. There were times when he ached for the comfort of a soft warm bed, when he wrestled with the demons of his own desires and wept with the pain of loneliness. He was haunted by the cries of the sea-birds which sounded so human as they called to him night and day.

This had been no easy journey, no escape from temptation. These last four years had, for him, been a journey of fire. For, as he wrestled with the reality of who he was and fought with the strange demons of his past, he had become wiser and gentler. More connected to God and to the created order.

He watched the line of white surf which pierced the darkness beyond the rocky outcrop. The tide flowed in each day, and as it did so, he tried to spend the hours in silent contemplation, allowing the waves of God's love and power to flow through him that in return his prayers and praises might be borne up to God by more than human breath. And then, as the tide stood still, he would focus his mind on the pool of God's tranquillity and prepare himself for visitors.

Some days he would hear them from a distance, laughing and joking as they climbed up Middle Worm to mock him. One day their sarcasm would be purified by regret. Sometimes people would come to waste his time. To ask him why he lived that way and to talk of worldly things. He never spoke to such as these, but prostrated himself before his little altar and prayed that God would remove them from his holy sanctuary.

But others, many others, came for help. Whoever they were, they had to accept him as he was. Whether kings of tribes or landless paupers, they had to sit cross-legged on the dusty floor beside him and wait. For some short space, at least, they had to enter his world, share his hardship and understand his sacrifice. The emptiness of his cell was a symbol of his emptying of self that God might be all and be in all.

And so they came, those looking for meaning, or healing or for answers to life's great mysteries, and some seeking to know God's presence in a wild and desolate land. Each of them sat cross-legged in front of the stone altar while Maidoc gazed up at his cross and met his Lord. When he was ready he would simply look at them, his blazing blue eyes giving permission to speak.

It was the rule that he would only talk about the things of God. He spoke rarely, but when he did many claimed that they heard the very voice of God. What he said had a power and authority which rang from town to town across the land. Disputes over land were settled before his altar. Sick children were anointed with holy oil. Kings decided whether to make peace or make war. Men wept over the cruelty of fate or the demoralising grind of poverty. The desolate found new strength to continue.

As he stared out at the sea and sky that new year's

night, the hermit prayed. He prayed for those who'd sat beside him in his musty cave over the year now gone, and he prayed for distant civilisations, emerging generations. Lives damaged by societies he would never know and broken by pressures he could never understand.

As he prayed that night he thought he heard them coming. Unknown travellers clambering across the mysteries of time, climbing over the rocky bridge from the mainland, scrambling up Middle Worm and edging down the grassy slope towards him.

This is the story of their coming, and this, ultimately, is the story of how Maidoc reached across the centuries to meet them.

CHAPTER 1
Millennium Eve

Worm's Head

Josh took the flaming torch and thrust it into the bonfire. The wood crackled and sparked into flame. It had been well doused with petrol from Marie's old yellow can. Within minutes the five-foot high pile of wood and saw-dust was blazing.

Josh brushed his hand through his short razor-cut black hair. His long sideburns looked somehow incongruous with such a short cut. He was olive-skinned, Italian looking, of stocky build and barely taller than five feet nine. He was wearing the thick woollen poncho that he'd bought in South America. He treasured it; in some deep way it made him feel secure.

He smiled at his kids, Jem and Pol, aged nine years and twenty months respectively, who were dancing excitedly in front of the fire. Josh loved bonfires. He'd loved them since boyhood. Fire connected him to primeval humankind, and to distant cultures long ago. He shielded his eyes with his outstretched hand.

It was one of those clear crisp nights when you could see distant galaxies. The seven of them were standing on the furthest point west. On the edge of Wales, the edge of Britain, the edge of Europe. Josh felt as though he was on the edge of the world. It was a place he liked to be, especially with his own small community around him.

Leaders need followers, and Josh had Marie, his

partner, who was snuggling close to him. She would follow him, for she believed in him and really loved him. She would follow him to the end of the earth. There were other followers, too. Scott, a man in his early forties with his partner Suse who were standing hand in hand and looking out to sea. And Jez, a thin withdrawn lad who was lying on his back and gazing up at the stars.

Other travellers came and went with great regularity. Some stayed for a week, others for a month. Some disappeared for ever while others returned at regular intervals. Their most frequent visitor was David Rushden, the political activist, whom Josh found troublesome. Josh was glad that he was away in London that millennium night.

The Worm, as it was called, was a rugged outcrop stretching a mile out into the Atlantic from the Gower Peninsula, one of the most spectacular pieces of coastline in all of Britain. It was a wild, isolated place, though only just a few miles along the coast from the bustling university city of Swansea.

The fire roared, lighting up the faces of Josh's little community. They had all opted for this primitive lifestyle, driven by a need to escape the numbing influences of Western culture. But it was a life lived in the raw elements, and they looked rough and unkempt. Living in tents on the Gower in winter was no picnic.

Josh's group was seeking some sense of connection with the mystic or some experience of the divine. In order to achieve this they believed that the higher self had to be aroused, for they understood that 'all is one, God is all, and all is God'.

Josh had taught them that the old epoch of rationalism was disappearing, and that the new age of 'knowing' was about to dawn. They were, as a community, preparing for the Age of Aquarius. He was the community's respected leader, someone whose rugged tenacity and exuberant personality won people over to follow him.

He put his arm around Marie, his latest partner, and squeezed her close to him. She was a quiet girl with long dark hair that reached to her waist, and which she hid behind when she felt embarrassed. She had a good figure and wore bright red jeans and yellow tops that brought colour to the most dismal surroundings. She exuded a warmth and motherliness which made Josh feel good.

They had met in a community in Cornwall the previous summer. Josh was struggling to bring up two daughters on his own, and she had seemed eager to help. It had been a beautiful love affair. The long summer days on the superb surf beaches near Newquay and the warm evenings of conversation beside a camp fire in a valley miles from anywhere.

Josh had been living with the group in Cornwall for over six months when Marie arrived. She was travelling alone, a free spirit, and living in an igloo tent which she carried in her rucksack. She was a confident surfer, the result of many summers surfing off Rhosili beach on the Gower. It had given her a wide experience of varied sea conditions which Josh couldn't match.

Their relationship had begun through the girls, Jem and Pol. Marie had always been good with kids. She'd practically brought up her two sisters alone, yet Jem and Pol had tested her to the limit. Josh had spoiled them as he'd tried to make up for the loss of Meena, their mother, and whenever Marie tried to instil some kind of discipline into them they just went wild.

She'd done her best to help Josh with them because he didn't have much idea of how to control their strong wills and determined attitudes. 'When you say no, mean no,' she'd urged him. 'The kids are just confused. You say "no", and then you just let them carry on. No wonder they're out of control.'

Gradually, however, Josh had come to love her. It was not simply a love based on physical attraction, for Marie was no stunning beauty. It was based on affection and on a sense of ease at being in each other's company. She'd moved the igloo tent next to Josh's tepee, and they had begun to cook together. Josh was an excellent cook, and the vegetarian curries which he concocted were the finest she'd ever tasted. Meena, his former partner, had taught him all that there was to know about curry.

One night in a torrential downpour Marie's igloo tent had leaked, and she'd found herself peering in through the tepee flap and asking for shelter. From that point on their relationship had moved onto a different level.

It had been Marie's idea to start a community of their own on the Gower. She knew the area well, and had grown up nearby. She'd always felt that it was a special place, a place where you could focus on things that were important. She told him that it had good karma and would be a place of safety in which to rear the girls.

Marie always knew that Josh would make a great leader. Without her affirmation and confidence in him, however, he would probably have never branched out on his own. He would always be indebted to her for believing in him.

They had arrived on the Gower only four months previously in early September, and had found a field to pitch camp in behind Anita Atwell's house. It wasn't perfect, but it was a start. The invisible networks of the New Age community had begun to operate, and soon Jez, Scott, Suse and Dave had come to join them. Sometimes there were as many as twenty others passing through.

'Can we go now, Dad?' moaned Jem.

'Go? No, of course we can't go. We've not welcomed in the new year yet,' muttered Josh firmly. He always knew his mind.

'Look, look over there,' said Marie in her lilting Welsh accent. 'It's another fire, isn't it?' She pointed out to sea. In the far distance glowed a flicker of orange light.

'Yep. That's the Devon beacon.' Josh felt part of some great company of people who were lighting beacons that night. 'You think they can see ours?'

'I reckon so. It's a perfect night.' Marie was gazing back along the coastline towards Swansea, wondering if there was a beacon there, too.

The sea was still and calm save for the distant whisper of the surf on the long sandy beach. Gulls were still wheeling overhead, stirred from the safety of their sanctuary by the leaping flames. Far above them was a vast parade of stars stretching out across the horizon and into infinity.

Jez lit a cigarette and lay on his back, puffing a long thin stream of smoke into the chill night air. 'There's the Plough, there, look. See it?'

They all gazed up. 'What are you looking at, what do you mean, the Plough?' nine-year-old Jem asked patiently.

Josh whisked her up into his arms and took her delicate hand in his. He pointed it upwards, gently drawing the outline of a plough against the pattern of the stars. 'It's like a plough, see? Like we saw on Ben's farm? They call that line of stars the Plough.'

'Daddy?' Pol was tugging at his trouser leg. She always had to be part of the action.

'In a minute, Pol. Just give us a minute.' There were times when Pol just wound him up.

Marie stooped down to lift the child into her arms, but Pol clung tightly to her father's leg. She didn't trust

Marie, and besides, she wanted her dad. Marie felt this rejection keenly, and it came from both girls in a hundred tiny ways each day.

'I wonder how Dave's getting on,' Marie said, to set aside the hurt she felt.

'He's a total berk. He'll get everything he deserves,' Josh muttered, still clutching Jem close to him.

Jez puffed a long stream of smoke into the air. 'Pity you didn't have the guts to go with him, like he asked you.'

'He's mad. He's totally lost it. He needs his head examining.' Josh sounded very sarcastic.

'But he's doing our thing. It's what we all believe in, but perhaps the rest of us haven't got the guts to go the whole way,' Jez retorted. Jez had hit a nerve.

Things between Josh and Dave had been deteriorating. They both shared a New Age perspective, but they disagreed profoundly on how it should be worked out in everyday life.

* * *

Only two days previously, David Rushden had been packed and ready to go to London. There were only two buses a day from Rhosili to Swansea, and he daren't miss the afternoon one. As he ambled through the orchard towards the gate with his bag over his shoulder, Josh called after him.

'I think you're wrong, Dave. You've overstepped the mark this time.' Dave turned and faced him.

'What do you mean?'

'This effing plan of yours. It's a different ball-park from picketing some building site or trying to save some trees. This is dangerous.' There was a note of real concern in his voice.

'You worry too much, Josh. It'll be fine. I'll take care.'

'I think you're doing us no favours. You'll just put people off. Why isn't it enough just to model what we believe?'

'No, it can't be enough. Not for me, anyway.' Dave turned to go.

Josh was starting to get angry. 'Why can't you live it day in and day out like the rest of us? Think small. Live community. Demonstrate simple lifestyle. Reject possessions. Abandon the motor car. Develop self-sufficiency. It's all here.'

Dave stopped, and strolled back towards Josh. 'It's not enough for me, Josh. The world needs changing. We've got to challenge the government, propagandise through the press.'

Josh approached him and drew himself up to his full height, but he still felt dwarfed by Dave's lanky stature. 'We've got a good thing going here. We can make a difference, to the Gower at least. If you get snarled up with the police you could ruin everything for us.'

'Take it easy. I'll keep you out of it.' He put down his bag.

'I'm not sure I trust you.' Josh sounded emotional. 'You've been trying to get the others to go with you behind my back, haven't you?'

Dave had had enough. He snatched his bag and slung it over his shoulder and turned to go. 'I'll see you in a couple of days.'

'If you go, you're not welcome back.'

Dave paused, he had his back to Josh. 'OK.'

'I'll pack up your things. You can just pick them up when you get back. You're going to bring trouble. I can sense it.'

Dave turned towards Josh, took him by the collar and pulled him close. 'You just dare touch my things.'

The community did share the same agenda. They all wanted to advance ecology, break down male-female distinctions, and tap into the world's healing processes. They all wanted to humanise technology, dismantle corporate Britain and develop a new way of living based in small industrial and agricultural collectives. It was just that Dave was more impatient. More of an activist. Willing to take the law into his own hands.

Dave let Josh go and looked at him disparagingly. 'The trouble with you, Josh, is that you're a passenger. You're just here for the ride, you don't really care.' Dave couldn't cope with the laissez-faire attitude which Josh applied to the whole of life and especially to the way he ran the community.

'And the trouble with you, Dave Rushden,' Josh retorted, 'is that you take the whole damn thing too seriously. Live a little, and let live.'

He had been finding Dave's attitude more and more oppressive. Josh was a free spirit, and he had no intention of being treated like a kid. Perhaps Dave's relationship with the community was over. Perhaps this was the moment when Josh should exercise his leadership once and for all.

Dave could hear the bus climbing up the hill towards Rhosili and he turned back towards the gate. Had it not been for the bus they might well have come to blows.

* * *

Out on the Worm on millennium night, Josh looked at Jez. His eyes were alight with anger. Jez returned the look. There was an awkward silence until Marie intervened.

'Leave it alone, Jez. You know it's a sore point. If you were so committed why didn't you go to London, too?' Marie sounded passionate, her Welsh lilt growing stronger. She was always defensive of Josh when he was under attack.

'OK, OK.' Scott, the older man in his mid-forties was, as ever, the calming influence. 'Just cool it. We're here to party, not to slag each other off.' Scott was committed to the New Age sense of unity in all things, and it irritated him that sometimes those who were part of the community seemed to have grasped so little about what that really meant in their everyday relationships.

The basic philosophy of the Gower community was that 'all is one'. They saw the cosmos as pure, undifferentiated, universal energy — a consciousness, or life force. There, on the edge of the world, it became something tangible. The community was a part of the stars, the sea, the birds, and each other. Life was all interconnected. Yet putting that philosophy into practice in everyday relationships was often demanding.

Jez stood, took one last drag from his cigarette, and flicked it into the air. It flew like a firefly onto the rocks below. The tension between him and Josh still hung heavy in the air.

Josh chucked another log onto the blazing bonfire. There was no wood on the Worm itself, so they had carried it from their camp. They had made journey after journey from the orchard where they lived, past the cottages and the Worm Hotel, and along the coastal footpath to the ridge which led to the rocky outcrop itself.

They had carried the loads of wood, piled high on top of an old door, whenever the tide had permitted them during the days since Christmas. Thankfully the weather had been mild, another indication, as Marie had told them, that global warming would soon bring

Mediterranean temperatures to the Gower all year round.

It had not been easy. The tide drifted in slowly over a period of six hours and then gently ebbed out again during the following six. Anyone who made the perilous journey out to the edge of the Worm had to time their departure and return very carefully.

The first wet rocks appear through the shipway between the Inner Head and the mainland about two and a half hours after high water. Anyone who is adventurous enough has five hours to cross the mile of rough rock to the far end of the Worm and get back again before the incoming tide. The latest point at which you can leave the island is three and a half hours before high water.

The rocky ridge out to the Worm is slimy and weed-covered and on the land-ward edge there is a field of tall water reeds. You must then climb the steep grassy hill of Middle Worm, and descend across Devil's Bridge to the rough rocky cliff known as Worm's Head. It is easy to miscalculate the journey, for if you take too long to reach the furthest perimeter of the Worm you can miss the tide on your return.

Many people have been stranded on Worm's Head over the years. The reeds at the edge of the rocky outcrop make the return journey look safer than it really is, and if you start the walk back along the rocky shelf too late you can be swept out to sea. Several people have drowned there in recent years.

Everyone in Josh's little community had helped to transport the wood, of course. At dawn each day, because of the early low tide, they had made a little procession with the old door piled high, and carried bags of sawdust from Jez's carpentry bench. There was enough wood there to keep the fire going for much of the night if necessary.

There had, of course, been other bonfires on

Worm's Head. Human remains which are more than 100,000 years old have been found there, and fire has always been a hallmark of human presence.

Josh had loved bonfires ever since he and his gang first started playing with matches on the common behind his parents' beautiful detached home in Winchester. It was a childhood which lacked for nothing except love and attention.

Josh poked the fire with a stick. For an instant, he wondered what it would have been like in those primeval times, lighting fires for warmth in rugged and desolate places like Worm's Head. It must have been a harsh kind of world, not too unlike the world of his community on the Gower.

Maybe men and women had stood on this very spot then, when the Worm was still indissolubly joined to the mainland, before tide and storm had eroded the bridge of land and made it impassable at high tide.

He smiled. In the vast expanse of history this second millennium celebration was rather a non-event. History was a strange phenomenon, sometimes so distant, yet often so closely connected. In the raw ruggedness of the place and the infinity of the night sky he sensed that those distant peoples were watching him. They had come to watch this new generation of explorers on the edge of the world who were searching for the interconnectedness of all things.

Josh was hungry for transcendence. He looked at Jem and Pol. They were the rising generation, flesh of his flesh. He wondered what kind of world they would inherit. He loved them, but struggled with his role as their father. He gazed down at Jem, her face lit up by the flickering firelight. She was dark and olive-skinned with big questioning brown eyes. She looked like Meena, her mother.

Meena was born in South India, and it was her grasp of Eastern mysticism and her intuitive sensitivity which had drawn Josh to her. They first met in a community in the New Forest, and soon came to love each other with unreserved passion. They had shared a tepee, and shared a life.

She would sit for hours cross-legged in front of the tepee as if in a trance. Her hands moved gently as if she was gathering some soft silken karma towards her. She saw everything as interconnected to the mystic stream of life.

'Josh, my lover, calm down,' she would say. Her Indian accent was gentle, and somehow reassuring. 'Your biorhythms are all over the place.'

Meena lived her life by biorhythms. She believed that the twenty-three day physical rhythm was rooted in the action of muscle fibres, and that it influenced Josh's physical strength, endurance and energy levels. His emotional rhythm, however, derived from the nervous system and manifested itself in emotional changes and degrees of sensitivity. Meanwhile, his intellectual rhythm originated in his brain cells, and it varied with the regular cycle which controlled him.

Meena measured the rise and fall of these three dominant rhythms in everyone around her. When, as occasionally occurred, two or more of the cycles reached a coincidental change-over she cautioned them to do nothing until the crisis was passed.

At first Josh had been mesmerised by her knowledge of such things, but as the years went by he had grown irritated by it all. Meena had become a slave to the obscure charts which registered the changing rhythms of herself and those around her. There were some days when she would do nothing and go nowhere because her rhythms were in change-over. Her addiction to the charts became more and more evident and Josh felt that her sensitivity to the mystic had become more important than her awareness of him.

Gradually their relationship deteriorated. It became tempestuous, full of loud arguments and intense reconciliations. She was too much a traveller to stay anywhere for long; constantly restless; always looking for another community to belong to and a greater sense of karma to experience. Her restlessness exhausted him.

Meena and Josh had shared a life together for nine years, but when Jem had her eighth birthday Meena had told him that it was time for her to move on. He had begged her to stay, pleaded with her to reconsider, but her mind was made up. Something within her was still restless, still unresolved, and she longed for India.

One night she simply disappeared. She left a note saying that she would always love them and carry them in her heart. Josh had never understood her decision, nor the sudden way in which she left. Mothers do not leave their children, and he felt she'd no right to leave Jem and Pol. Josh carried an unresolved sense of anger and betrayal about it all.

At first he had waited for her to return but he gradually found the months of silence heart-breaking. He even wondered whether she was still alive. Slowly, he tried to overcome his painful sense of loss.

He had found the girls more of a burden than he'd ever imagined. Josh was the only security in Jem and Pol's unsettled little world and they loved him intensely, but Jem still missed her mum and often cried herself to sleep at night. Pol was a bundle of energy and demanded his undivided attention during every waking hour. Marie had arrived to help him just when he'd reached breaking point.

Josh threw another log on the fire. He had felt it right to celebrate the millennium here on the Worm because of its undisputed links with history.

In the roaring flames he saw the bonfires of the Vikings. Tall flaming lighthouses built to guide their ships towards the vast sandy beach of Rhosili Bay for the great invasion of 1089. The Vikings were a wild, hard people, come to raid the scores of churches in the area. Later they would penetrate further inland to attack the shrine of St David and to steal its gold and silver. Even as he looked through the darkness at the shimmering silver sea he could imagine their sturdy ships, so ornately carved, rounding the headland and guided to safety by the beacon of fire burning brightly on the Worm.

Time was a strange phenomenon. Josh looked at his little community and wondered why they were all together in such a time and place. Some New Agers would argue that they were a reincarnation of another group from a distant age. Others believed that death was an individual passage to cyclical but unending rebirth. The subject fascinated him. Perhaps he was a reincarnation of some Viking warrior who in turn had been a member of the ancient Celtic community on the Gower. He often mused about life and immortality, and wondered in what incarnation he might return to earth.

There had been other bonfires on Worm's Head, of course, bonfires built by the smugglers of the sixteenth century. The headland was far enough from civilisation to make it safe, yet the rocky protrusion could be clearly seen at sea.

Those reckless men had risked their very lives for priceless contraband. They had burnt timber on the Worm to signal passing ships. It was a useful point of reference for unloading booty into small boats at sea. Once transferred, the illegal barrels of liquor were brought into the secluded coves at Pwll Ddu and Brandy Cove. These rugged inlets were only accessible by foot and were shielded by cliffs which towered more than two hundred feet above. Maybe he, Josh Lake, had lived the life of a smuggler then.

The isolated coastline around the Worm had proved an ideal haunt for smugglers. Even now, in their encampment nearby, Josh felt that he and his community were remote enough from civilisation to escape the law. The Gower was a kind of no-man's land, as useful a hideaway today as it has always been.

He looked out towards the distant darkness and wondered if anyone had lit a fire on Lundy Island, twenty-three miles to the south. But there was nothing there except the dark line of the horizon. The sea seemed to stretch for ever beneath the starlit sky.

As Josh looked into the leaping flames of his millennium bonfire he pictured the kaleidoscope of other bonfires on the edge of Worm's Head. But there was one bonfire he did not picture, a small smoky fire lit by one solitary figure. A hermit called Maidoc.

There, just where Josh and the others had built their bonfire, Maidoc had lit his small fire each Easter Saturday. Maidoc, the hermit of Worm's Head, with his long tousled hair and bushy brown beard, had lit a fire that was as important to him as a holy sacrament. He was following an ancient tradition brought first to Wales by some Christians with the Roman Army. The fire of Holy Saturday.

Maidoc was a broad well-built man. He wrapped himself around with the thick brown woollen habit that was his most precious possession, and sat alone beside his fire each Holy Saturday. He recited his litany of prayers, shouting loudly above the wheeling seabirds circling overhead, and thanking God for the sacrifice of his Son.

When his prayers were finished, Maidoc took a torch made out of twigs and rags and plunged it into his fire. He carried the flaming symbol back over the rocky path of Devil's Bridge, up the steep hill of Middle Worm, and scrambled down the grassy bank and into his hermit's cave.

He bent low to reach the inner cave, still carrying the flaming torch, and joyfully lit the candles lined up in waiting rows on the stony ledge that was his altar. Soon the darkness was gone and the cave blazed with flickering light. He lay prostrate before the blazing altar and cried, 'Jesus is the light of the world. He is risen! He is risen! He is risen indeed!'

Josh stoked the fire again and a flurry of sparks showered over the cliff edge and into the darkness below. Those bonfires on Worm's Head were like flaming torches which passed from culture to culture; from generation to generation. Josh was mesmerised by the thought of them. He wondered if he'd been a part of those other times or if, perhaps, those other times were part of him.

It was somehow reassuring that as civilisations came and went that Worm's Head stood firm against the battering of wind and tide. Josh gazed out across the calm still sea which shimmered in the silver moonlight and felt enfolded by eternity. In that moment, he felt that time and timelessness were one.

* * *

Rhosili village

Just over a mile away from the big bonfire on the Worm, in one of the string of slate-roofed cottages next to the

Worm Hotel, Anita Atwell sat in her wheelchair. She was looking out of her tall veranda windows at the waves shimmering in the moonlight.

What did she hope for on millennium night? The question rolled around her mind, it was certainly a night for hopes and dreams. To walk again. That would be her greatest dream. But the consultant had told her to stop hoping. 'Multiple sclerosis may go into remission,' he had said, 'but it rarely goes away.'

She'd had to give up primary teaching in the twenty-fifth year of her career and the forty-sixth year of her life, and it had been a blow from which she'd never fully recovered. She could have coped, perhaps, with the illness alone, but the loss of her vocation was just too much to bear.

Anita had never married, though when she was nineteen she'd once been in love. It had been a heady affair, and very romantic. Stephen was in his final year at college when she was only a fresher, and they had met in the college choir.

She had never felt good about herself but somehow Stephen had made her feel wanted, special — even beautiful. York was a beautiful place to study, and they had both relished the sense of history and culture which permeates the whole city.

They had spent many weekends hiking around the Yorkshire Dales, exploring quaint villages like Leyburn and Bedale. They had stood in solemn amazement within the ruins of Fountains Abbey, walked hand in hand beside Aysgarth Falls, and discovered wonderful teashops in the old town of Richmond. It had been the kind of relationship of which she'd always dreamed. They shared a common love of history and a fascination with the spectacular scenery of Wensleydale. They also shared a depth of faith which was rooted in traditional Anglicanism.

After graduating Stephen had moved to teach in a private school in Oxfordshire, and was soon engrossed in school life. The letters arrived regularly at first, and they had arranged to spend half term together. As she was packing to leave, however, a letter arrived which told her of a change of plan. It signalled the end of everything. It was a letter which broke her heart and sapped her confidence. No one else had ever lived up to him.

Why hadn't she married? The question haunted her, and she frequently tried to answer it. Was it because she was 'plain' and had no confidence in her appearance, or that the man she truly loved had rejected her? She often wondered, and still carried deep and lasting regrets.

Following a couple of rather disastrous relationships which had left her feeling used, she resolved that she would never marry, but give her life to teaching. She took a job in a multi-racial school in Brixton, a school with one of the most unfortunate reputations in London. Her teaching became an obsession, a crusade, a cause; and she invested all her emotional and physical energy into it.

She could have climbed the ladder of promotion, of course, but she fiercely resisted any offer which took her out of the classroom. Her commitment to each year's class of eight-year-olds was complete. She gave of her very best, often working long into the night to prepare her lessons.

On Sundays she attended the early service at her local Anglican church. Her faith revolved around the 1662 prayerbook and a sense of reliable structure in worship. Anita was a spiritual woman, but until her illness she'd never had the time or energy to invest in it.

Anita looked out of her window and watched spellbound as each new wave slowly built and then paused for an instant, as if reaching up towards the moon, before exploding into a sheet of white spray racing towards the beach.

She leant back in her wheelchair and stared out at the distant outline of the Worm, snake-like against the dim silver of the sea. There, on Worm Head, she could see the bonfire's leaping flames. They had done it, they had built a bonfire to welcome the new millennium. How she longed to be out there with them, with Josh and Marie, and Scott and Suse and Jez. She longed to see Jem's excited face, and to nurse little Pol tight in her arms. She'd come to love this little community so much.

When, two years before, the doctor had told her to quit teaching and start looking after herself, she had wrestled with the limited options before her. She could enter sheltered accommodation in London, and still maintain links with the children and teachers at the school. Or she could move to Rhosili, the village on the Gower, and the cottage left to her in her aunt's last will and testament.

It had been a difficult decision, and one which she had wrestled with over many sleepless nights. She loved the children and followed their progress with the keenest interest, but something within her felt uncomfortable about remaining in London. Perhaps, after all, they would soon forget her and she would find herself feeling cheated that she could no longer play an active role in the life of the school. She resolved to branch out and begin again. It was a brave decision for her at forty-six and on her own. Especially as the only real prospect was one of declining health.

Eighteen months had passed since her final leaving party at the school in July 1998. A joyous celebration of all her years of caring. They had come back from all over the country, over two hundred of them, to say thank you. It was the happiest and saddest day of her life all rolled into one. The years she had invested in them had been worth while, and she felt richly rewarded by their love and appreciation.

The move to the Gower had been traumatic. Moving house when she was in good health would have been one thing, but her every joint ached and throbbed and it had been a nightmare. If it hadn't been for the folk from Rhosili church she might never have unpacked at all. As it was, the Women's Institute had adopted her as a special project . . . and had helped her unpack and get sorted out with their usual efficiency.

Life at Rhosili hadn't been easy. Anita had grown up in South Wales, but had never lived anywhere as tiny or as remote as this. The people had been friendly enough at first, but as time went by she found herself becoming increasingly isolated. It was probably her own fault. It's not easy to relate to Welsh village culture when you're used to cosmopolitan Brixton.

Her sense of connection with the created order had developed as she gazed out at the view from her window. The view of the Worm had helped her to focus on God. Gradually she had begun to discover a spiritual side to her life and to explore a new sense of the mystery of God. She owed it all to Maidoc, her Celtic hero.

She had first heard of him through the Rhosili church newsletter. The church at Llanmadoc with Cheriton and Llanrhidian was having a feast day for its patron saint, and the congregation at Rhosili was running a minibus to the festivities. She had somehow struggled aboard and made her five-mile pilgrimage to Llanmadoc.

It was the smallest church on the Gower, and in some ways the most historic. Set into the window-sill of the first window there was a Romano-British tombstone which was discovered by the rector in 1861. It simply read, 'The stone of Advectus, son . . . Guanus. He lies here.' It dated from the sixth century. Beside it was a Celtic cross of even greater antiquity.

There had been a pleasant tea followed by a choral concert and evening prayer. On her way back in the minibus Anita Atwell had promised herself to find out who Maidoc was, and what he had done. It turned out to be a far greater challenge than she had imagined, and had it not been for the regular visits of the mobile library and the enthusiastic young girl who ran it she might never have discovered Maidoc the hermit.

Over the weeks that followed, however, the mobile library brought her an assortment of books unlike any others ever requested by its readers. Mainly they were books from the University of Swansea's Celtic Studies Unit. Books about the Celtic saints, books which mentioned Maidoc.

Anita discovered that Maidoc had withdrawn to the Worm — the rocky outcrop so clearly visible from her veranda window. But he had not withdrawn to escape a world of suffering, but to confront it. Maidoc was not an aristocrat, like some of the other Celtic hermits, but the son of a carpenter. Following the death of his young wife in childbirth, Maidoc had committed himself to a life of asceticism and tireless prayer.

He went first to Ireland to learn in one of the Irish monasteries founded by Brendan, and then returned to Wales to follow a life of solitude. It was not an escape, but a means of journeying towards God. He had made a conscious decision not to be attached to anybody or anything, that he might become completely attached to Jesus Christ and discover true connection with his universal love.

Maidoc lived the hermit life on Worm's Head for four years but then moved to the hamlet now known as Llanmadoc to found a congregation and a simple monastery of his own. He became quite crotchety in old age, and could not abide the sound of music. He always carried two balls of wax with him, Anita read with amusement, to plug his ears against the sound of any music he might hear. After hearing the music of heaven he could no longer abide the music of earth.

Anita was fascinated by the man and sensed that in some strange providential way she had come to Rhosili to continue his work. She knew that she couldn't build a spirituality based solely on the insights, prayers, rituals, myths, symbols and devotional practices of her Celtic hero. Yet she found that she could draw on the richness of his tradition and recover precious insights which the Church had lost.

Maidoc's Celtic spirituality, which she took as her model, majored on a sense of the abiding presence of Christ. She discovered that Maidoc was a man intoxicated with God and embraced by love. He connected to God through the wonders of nature and through seeing Christ's presence in every aspect of creation.

Anita searched for that intensity of faith and yearned to be connected to that unitive force which holds creation together. She longed to understand people more fully and to know the reality behind life itself — the cosmic Christ.

Anita Atwell had left teaching behind and taken on a new challenge. It was as demanding as teaching, though its results were not easily demonstrable nor recognised by the world. Like Maidoc, fifteen hundred years before her, Anita had made this corner of the Gower peninsula her place of contemplation. Her place of struggle. Her place of tears. Like Maidoc before her, she prayed that God would bring the needy to her sanctuary that she might pray for them and show them compassion.

Her decision to join the Sisters of the Seashore was

not taken lightly. It wasn't a cop-out, or a way of turning her back on the past. It was a way of moving forward and of finding fulfilment. It had become the key to the next phase of her life. With Maidoc as her inspiration, and this loosely connected community of praying Christians as her guide, she had embarked on a journey of prayer and intercession.

In the early days she had felt intensely lonely, and she prayed that somehow God would take that away. After fourteen months of asking, the prayer was answered one fine September day when Josh Lake knocked on her door. The day when her orchard became a haven for such unlikely guests.

*   *   *

Whitehall, London

David Rushden was standing on the pavement outside the entrance to Horseguard's Parade in Whitehall, London. He had never felt so scared or so excited in his life. The fourteen members of his team were gathered tightly around him and he was whispering their final instructions in short rapid phrases. Passing by were hordes of new year revellers, and there was a buzz of excitement in the air.

His long dark hair was tied back into a pony tail, but strands of it were dancing over his forehead in the gentle breeze. Over his shoulder was slung his ornately patterned cloth bag, and inside it was a long piece of thick rope. His denim shirt and jeans and faded jacket were worn and patched.

Dave was tall, over six feet two, yet there was a gentleness about him which made him approachable and easy to talk to. He exuded a kind of confidence and trustworthiness which made him a natural leader. When he looked at you, he listened and, because he listened, he somehow understood.

Dave's career in political action had started innocently enough when he had taken part in an ecology march organised by the National Union of Students in Manchester. He'd met some interesting people, the kind of oddball individuals he'd normally never have mixed with. Most of them were studying sociology, politics and philosophy. They seemed altogether a wilder set than the boffins he worked with each day in the rather dour physics department.

They'd invited him to spend the summer on an eco protest in a Somerset forest. There he'd met Eva, an intense and passionate girl with a vivacious personality and an ebullient sense of humour who welcomed him into a community of fellow travellers committed to the New Age.

Eva had taught him how to connect with the ancient mysteries of pre-Christian religion and had encouraged him to reach out towards new alternative forms of mysticism. He had become a child of the New Age. She had shown him how to centre his life in the heart, and how to touch that source by which the intellect is activated. He had come to believe that a true love for all humanity could only proceed from a knowledge of his true self, and he had applied himself to acquiring that knowledge for more than eight years.

Dave had loved Eva with an intensity which frightened him. He had never known love like it before and feared that he'd never know it again. They'd shared a love for life and for the earth which made each day an exciting childhood adventure. Through her he came to find a new joy for living and a new sense of beauty in the world. In her presence things lit up in new ways. Life took on a heady new excitement. And there was laughter, always laughter.

Under Eva's influence Dave became a core member of Mother Earth, a group committed to ecology. They believed that the society of the new millennium must protect the sensitively connected ecosystems of the planet or face apocalyptic consequences. The group blamed contemporary technology for many of the world's worst eco-disasters. The oil industry and the car were, as far as they were concerned, the most destructive forces in the world. True enemies of the people.

David Rushden was looking for a future focused on the development of small integrated communities, a greater sense of connection with nature, more sharing, and a deep care for the environment. It was as yet only a hope and a dream. One day, he knew that it would become reality. He owed it all to Eva, and even as he continued briefing his team for the daring demo ahead, he felt that she was standing there too. Her big blue eyes were looking at him, as if to ask him why. He owed it all to her. But he ached that she wasn't there on millennium night to share in his moment of triumph.

* * *

The three police cars and the white crewbus which made up Alpha Four were standing by near Charing Cross Bridge. The fourteen members of the squad had been waiting for over an hour. Crowds of people were streaming past them towards Trafalgar Square. Time was dragging by, and the crew sat silent and tense as the minutes passed.

John Breeson, driver of the lead car, was looking through the front windscreen. He didn't like the new year shift, it had a habit of turning nasty. He watched a gang of teenage lads ambling across the road in front of them. Some of them were already much too rowdy for his liking.

Alpha Four had been told to keep as low a profile as possible or else Breeson would have lifted some of the lads there and then. He dreaded what they would become in the next two hours after they'd consumed the large quantities of lager that they were carrying in handy twelve-can packs.

* * *

Back at Horseguards', David Rushden looked around at the knot of roughly dressed men and women gathered tightly around him. No one spoke, but they looked at him with trusting eyes. He had earned their respect through many courageous campaigns. They knew he wouldn't let them down.

Mother Earth was a very ad-hoc organisation. It had no formal structure, but drew over a hundred eco-warriors into a loose kind of active partnership. They only met when they were engaged in radical action. There were no membership lists or subscription fees, just a network of relationships revolving round the New Age communities in the south.

David Rushden was one of their most respected leaders. He combined a total commitment to eco-issues with a military precision which meant that his campaigns generally made headlines and got results. Above all, they knew that David Rushden was a pacifist. He always turned away from violence because it meant bad karma.

Dave put out his clenched fist. Without hesitation the others reached out their right hands and made a tower of fists resting on top of his. As soon as they were all joined Dave smiled confidently.

'Just do it,' he said softly.

The hands separated, and they dispersed into the seething crowds streaming up Whitehall. It was very noisy and they quickly vanished among the throng. Dave set out towards Downing Street, pushing his way against the stream of people heading for Trafalgar Square. He felt sure of victory, and there was confidence in every step.

If David Rushden lived anywhere, he lived with the small community of New Age travellers in the rough camp in Anita Atwell's orchard. There wasn't much there, just a few tents, tepees and huts, but it was the place he most fequently went back to and he looked on it as home. He was sad that Josh, the leader of the community, had refused to join him in London, and that Josh had forbidden the other members of the community to get involved. It was a constant disappointment to Dave that, although Josh had wholeheartedly adopted the New Age lifestyle he couldn't see that political action and good propaganda were part of the same package.

Dave stood before the tall gates of Downing Street. He remembered the time when, as a boy, he'd walked up Downing Street with his class from school and posed for a picture in front of Number Ten. Those days were long gone. The Prime Minister's residence was now a minor fortress.

Dave's heart was beating rapidly. He glanced at his watch. Three minutes to go. Josh should be here now, he thought. Not lighting some bonfire by the sea. That would do no good. If the world was really going to be changed, someone somewhere had to take the initiative. It was too easy for Josh to escape into a lifestyle as irresponsible and self-centred as that of the most materialistic suburbanite. It was all very well for Josh to model an alternative way of life, but his easy-going passivity would never change the world.

Somewhere in the distance, Big Ben struck quarter past eleven. Dave was breathing rapidly now, his breath rose like steam in the chill night air. He felt his heart pounding. There was a surge of excitement within him. He looked to his right and left. The other four were in place. He took a long deep breath and dived towards the gates.

* * *

'Stand-by Alpha Four.'

Breeson lifted the handset to his ear. 'Major disturbance at Downing Street. Proceed immediately.'

'Alpha Four. Message received. Logged at 23:23 hours.' John Breeson passed the handset to the sergeant beside him and started the engine. The instruction came as a relief. He didn't like the waiting.

The four vehicles wound their way down London's famous riverside Embankment, sirens wailing. Sergeant Stephens, seated in the front passenger seat, leant forward and spoke into the handset.

'Which approach?' he muttered, already trying to work out the best route through the maze of traffic ahead.

The sirens wailed as the four vehicles edged their way forward. There were thousands of pedestrians at every road junction. The fourteen policemen who made up the complement of Alpha Four were silent. There was always trouble on New Year's Eve, but this sounded more ominous, and perhaps more dangerous.

John Breeson was starting to sweat. The Embankment was a sea of people, and no one seemed interested in hurrying. The wail of the siren seemed totally ineffective. People just smiled and waved. This was a night for parties, not policemen.

* * *

Dave Rushden was already half-way up the eleven foot gate which provided the main security barrier between Whitehall and Downing Street. He was determined to get over it.

A policeman was grasping at his heels, but he kicked himself free and kept on climbing. The loop of rope he'd thrown over the top gave him extra purchase. He was fitter than ever, he'd been training for this moment for months.

He felt a buzz of exhilaration as his plan gradually unfolded. A dream becoming reality. The first wave of climbers was already on the gate, and two more groups of five were preparing to climb below. The assault was timed to start at four-minute intervals.

With fifteen of them on the gates, and the gates roped together, they hoped to lock the Prime Minister and his Cabinet inside their compound. It was so simple, yet potentially so effective.

All fifteen had been training hard. The two policemen inside the gate and the two outside were unprepared and overwhelmed. Yet the two outside the gate had managed to arrest one member of the first group who was now securely handcuffed to the railings in Whitehall.

The protest was carefully timed. If they could prevent the cortege of limousines from going through those gates, even for fifteen minutes, they could create mayhem. The Prime Minister, following dinner with the Cabinet in Downing Street, was to give a new millennium speech beside the Greenwich Meridian just after midnight. If he failed to turn up, Dave and the team would have scored a propaganda coup of international proportions.

Even as the third and final wave of climbers emerged from the stream of pedestrians on their way to Trafalgar

Square, the next phase of the operation was triggered. Some fifty protesters moved out of the crowd, linked arms, and sat cross-legged facing the two large black gates.

* * *

The four police vehicles edged their way round Parliament Square and slowly past the grim, determined statue of Winston Churchill standing guard over the city. The sirens were blaring, but inside the vehicles there was silence. The prospect of facing a riot is daunting, even for the most hardened copper.

The commander had considered that the complement of an inspector and three officers in charge of perimeter security at Downing Street was quite adequate. No intelligence had been received which indicated that there would be trouble there that night. Besides, with the plain clothes team from the Prime Minister's Protection Unit safely ensconced within Number Ten, there was a relatively strong police presence in the area.

The Protection Unit wasn't much use in this situation, however, because they had to remain with the PM at all times and would not leave the house until it was safe to escort him out. The commander would have to draw in other officers to tackle the problem.

Most of the uniformed officers at the commander's disposal were stationed behind the National Gallery in Trafalgar Square. It would be impossible to get them through a crowd of thirty thousand people in party mood. He also had surveillance teams near the Greenwich Meridian celebration and at an ethnic street party in Peckham which intelligence had reported might become the target for a racist attack . . . but they were too far away to respond to this. On a night like this trouble could happen anywhere.

The four vehicles of Alpha Four pulled up at the back of Downing Street beside St James's Park. It had been a tortuous journey. Sergeant Stephens stood beside the crewbus handing out crash hats and flack jackets. The fourteen members of the team scrambled up the grassy slope and through a black garden gate which gave private access to Downing Street. It was held open by an inspector whose uniformed detail had been in charge of perimeter security there. It had been a bad night and he was evidently relieved to see them.

Alpha Four's training had taught them to do nothing until instructed, and even then, to do no more and no less. They waited outside Number Twelve in a line, tense and breathless. The inspector was the senior policeman at the incident and he barked his orders in rapid-fire succession.

'Task one. Arrest anyone who has breached perimeter security and get them on the ground. Task two. Assist in opening gates. Task three. Carve a path through the demo line so that the limos can pass. Understood?'

As one they replied 'Sir.'

* * *

Jan Riley over at Connections Radio was coming up to her first scheduled report from Trafalgar Square, but Mike, the duty reporter, had found something more newsworthy on his way there. She pushed the 'outside source' fader to maximum.

'Hello there Mike, you're outside Downing Street, what's the story?'

'Well, Jan, a well-organised protest at Downing Street seems to have caught the police off guard. Already about five protesters have climbed onto the perimeter gates protecting Downing Street, but right now a team of trained riot control officers are advancing on the gates from within the compound. About six of the protesters have been arrested. Several of the officers are climbing the gates to pull down the remaining intruders and are cutting their ropes which have tied the gates shut. I'm told that they have four minutes to clear this demonstration or else the PM will miss his deadline at the Greenwich Meridian. The police are certainly not wasting any time.'

'What's the protest about?'

'Well, there are a lot of other people here in Whitehall with placards that seem to be accusing the government of a poor record on environmental issues.'

* * *

David looked down from his perch on top of the gate. He was almost four metres above the gazing crowd below. He reached to the back of his head and pulled out the band that held his hair. Suddenly his great mane of wiry black hair flowed free. He shook his head. Somewhere overhead a police helicopter hovered, its piercing searchlight focussed on him. He looked imposing, regal, like some ancient prophet from another time and another place. He smiled down at the fifty or more members of Mother Earth who were now in position. They were seated, cross-legged, in a line facing the gates. They were all looking up at him.

This was his moment, and the moment in which his Mother Earth movement had come of age. Cameras were flashing, and the first TV crew van was pulling up outside. This was the moment when he would challenge the world to make a new start for a new millennium. Josh had been wrong to try and stop him. So wrong.

Dave clung onto the gates for grim life. He imag-

ined himself standing in front of a major press conference. He was speaking and, at last, they were listening.

'Britain needs co-operation not competition, spon-
taneity not regulation, creativity not restriction. We must
protect creation instead of exploiting and destroying the
Earth's resources. We live in a global village. Britain must
stop functioning in isolation.'

This was his moment. The moment when Mother
Earth would speak to the world. How he wished that Josh
could see him now. This was the way. They could make a
difference. What good would Josh ever do hiding away in
the middle of nowhere? There was work to be done and a
war to be waged.

The three officers from Alpha Four climbing up
towards Dave knew exactly what they were doing. Two of
them pulled aggressively at his leg. He tried desperately to
cling on. A third policeman reached out, clasped his
hand, and jumped down from the gate, wrenching Dave's
hand down with him. It was just too much, he overbal-
anced, he couldn't stop himself. Dave knew that he was
falling. It was a fall which seemed to take a lifetime.

As he fell he sensed that he was falling from one
world to another. It only took a split second but it lasted
for ever. In that instant he faced the emptiness he had felt
for so long and his sadness over losing Eva. He was disconnected from the old as he fell towards the new.

Dave hit the ground with a loud crack as the back
of his head struck the tarmac. He shook violently just for
a moment and then lay still and unconscious. Gradually
a pool of blood gathered around his head.

Alpha Three, another of the six Metropolitan
Police riot squads on duty that night, had arrived in
Whitehall. They had taken a circuitous route from
behind the National Gallery to Hyde Park and past
Buckingham Palace and around Westminster Square.

They were beginning to disperse the protesters who were seated in front of the gates. Those who refused to move were carried to the side and handcuffed to the railings.

The inspector inside Downing Street looked at Dave's motionless body and then at his watch.

'Drag him out of the way,' he barked, 'NOW!'

Dave should not have been moved until expert medical help arrived, but the limo drivers were already starting their engines, and six motorcycle outriders were riding up Whitehall ready to escort the entourage to Greenwich. The door of Number Ten was open, and the VIPs were approaching their vehicles.

'NOW, I said, NOW.'

PC John Breeson and Sergeant Stephens looked at each other. They knew that what they had been ordered to do ran contrary to everything in their training. Breeson read his sergeant's eyes. It would be OK. They pulled Dave's limp body by the arms, and as they dragged him out of the way his head hung back and a stream of blood oozed out. It left a thin red trickle along the roadway of Downing Street.

The three limousines carrying the Prime Minister and members of the cabinet pulled swiftly and silently out of Downing Street. The large metal gates swung shut. The outriders wailed their way down Whitehall and into the distance. Gradually, order was being restored.

Inside Downing Street all those who had scaled the perimeter fence were now lying, face down, on the pavement outside Number Eleven. Eight policemen surrounded them, one armed.

The police were in no mood to make things easy, and when any of the protesters dared to move they screamed abusively at them. Later they would be cautioned and sent to three different police stations in central London for processing. They would all spend millennium night in the cells.

It took ten minutes for the ambulance to arrive to collect Dave, and the gates slowly swung open to allow it to pass through. Two attendants leapt out and quickly got to work on measuring his vital signs. A bright halogen spotlight mounted above the ambulance's rear doors cast harsh shadows as they worked.

It was clear that he had a nasty head injury, and as he wasn't conscious they took no chances. Within minutes he was encased within a large red neck collar support, which ran from beneath his shoulders to the top of his head. Two heavy waterbags were positioned on either side of his head, and his forehead was taped securely to them. With great care the two attendants, assisted by Sergeant Stephens, gently turned Dave's body while PC Breeson slid the scoop stretcher into place.

They loaded him into the brightly lit interior of the ambulance and PC John Breeson climbed in and sat facing him. There was no way that David Rushden was going anywhere without a police escort that night. Sergeant Stephens slammed the door shut and hit the back of the vehicle twice with the palm of his hand, as if to speed it on its way. Slowly it wailed out through the gates of Downing Street, past the stream of pedestrians in Whitehall and on towards St Thomas's hospital.

St Thomas's is a large complex beside the River Thames opposite the House of Commons, about a mile from Downing Street. Saint Tom's, as it's affectionately known, has the best Accident and Emergency Unit in central London and all the diagnostic equipment for suspected head and spinal injuries like David Rushden's.

As they unloaded the stretcher under the large brightly lit canopy of St Thomas's Accident and Emergency entrance and placed it onto a trolley, Dave opened his eyes. He felt a surge of panic ripping through him.

PC Breeson, hardened by his three years in the force, peered over. 'Good evening sunshine . . . are you with us, then? You might as well kiss the new millennium goodbye!' He sounded sarcastic.

The receptionist did her best to extricate the necessary information from Dave, but it was futile. Finally, her admission form still blank, she rolled her eyes in exasperation and waved the trolley on. She suspected that he was just playing games.

Dave Rushden looked blank. What had happened to him? And why couldn't he move? He lay on his back as the trolley was wheeled down an interminably long corridor. He looked at the strip lights skimming past overhead and wondered where they were taking him.

Within minutes the young houseman, Jane Jennings, swung into the cubicle and started to give him a Glasgow coma score—a detailed examination designed to identify the severity of his head injury. Somewhere in the distance there was a party going on. There were a lot of people laughing and talking. Who were these people? What was this celebration? And why was he in hospital?

CHAPTER 2

Millennium Midnight

Westminster Abbey. London

It was 11.25 pm at Westminster Abbey and James Roberts was feeling stressed. He didn't like doing media at the best of times, and he hadn't really wanted to do an interview in the minutes before the special millennium service at the Abbey. But the Dean insisted, and when the Dean insisted you were expected to comply.

Roberts sat alone in the robing room between the choir vestry and the clerical vestry. He was a tall man and he breathed confidence even when tightly knotted inside. Before him stood a table on which perched the Dean's latest toy — an ISDN link which gave a broadcast quality signal to any radio station in the country which cared to call him for an interview.

The contraption looked like a conventional phone stuck on the top of a large white plastic box. It was all set up with a white light to show that the line was open. All James had to do was talk when the red light flashed. He settled the earphones on his head and swivelled the tiny headset microphone so that it was just in front of his mouth.

He sat back and looked at the six wardrobes in front of him. One for each of the three Canons, one for the Chaplain, and two for the Dean. What a lot of wardrobes. What a lot of robes. He roundly detested the paraphernalia of institutional religion. The room smelt damp and musty, and it had a sad air of neglect. This was a part of the Abbey not generally seen by the public.

Roberts adjusted his cassock, he was only wearing it because he had to. He loosened the new MA degree hood hanging tightly round his neck. Despite his dislike for ceremonial robes he was proud of his hood. The MA had taken him hundreds of hours of painstaking research, and he had only been awarded it in October. It symbolised far more than his academic achievement, however, for his MA research had changed his life.

The light on the box flashed red and he shifted the microphone to check it was in place, making many thousands of unseen listeners flinch.

Jan Riley, anchor of the late-night show on Connections, a national chat and music station, was in full flow. 'And so we go live to Westminster Abbey, and welcome the Reverend James Roberts . . . is that your title?'

'Venerable, actually.'

'Oh, venerable?' Jan could hardly hide the sarcasm in her voice. She didn't like clergy. She never had.

'Yes, I'm Archdeacon of Wandsworth.' He had a deep resonant voice, with the faintest hint of a Geordie accent.

'So, you've been in charge of the Church's millennium celebrations for London?'

'Yes, that's right,' James said warmly, 'the Bishop knew that I was interested in history.'

'Tell us about the service, Archdeacon . . . it's celebrating the millennium?'

'Yes. It is. It's very exciting. We've got representatives from all the major Church traditions here. We've got Baptists, and the Salvation Army, and a few Pentecostals . . . and of course, the Catholics.'

'That's nice,' Jan could barely hide her contempt,

'but what about the other faith communities, have you included them?'

James smiled. He'd been anticipating this one. 'Naturally, we're delighted to have the spiritual leaders from the Moslem, Buddhist, Jewish and Bahai faiths. And they're all taking part.'

'And what about the Jehovah's Witnesses, the Mormons and the Scientologists, are they there too?'

'Oh no, of course not, I mean to say, they're all sects . . . . ' Roberts trailed off uncomfortably.

Jan smiled wryly. 'Sects?' She made it sound like sex.

'I'm sure they're having their own celebrations.' James felt uncomfortable.

Somewhere outside police sirens were wailing. A weird disturbing sound. There were several of them, but there was no harmony between them, just a jarring urgency.

'But why are you celebrating the millennium?' Jan was leading him gently into a trap.

'Because we are celebrating the coming of Christ, the change from BC to AD. It's essentially a Christian celebration.'

Jan smiled. 'But historians think the date's four years out, don't they?'

'That's as maybe, but it marks an important part of history so we'll celebrate it when we can.' James was growing irritated.

'But wouldn't this be a good time to drop the whole BC and AD thing, and move over to BCE — Before Common Era — like they teach in some schools?'

'Well, I'm not sure about that.'

There was a pause. Jan sometimes allowed pauses. They helped to create an atmosphere. She could clearly hear the sirens. They were so loud it was as if they were driving through the Abbey itself.

'Perhaps you'd like to check out the idea with some of your leaders from other faiths? Might make an interesting conversation?'

James was dumbstruck. He ran his hand through his dark shiny hair. There was a shade of grey around his temple. He looked mature, but there was still a youthfulness in his face, a kind of innocence, unusual in a man approaching fifty. He was transfixed. He wanted to talk about the service.

'But this really is an important act of worship, you know.' He tried to take control.

Jan smiled again. 'Isn't it the last gasp of a moribund Church?'

James felt anger rising. He gripped the table in front of him and struggled to sound warm and in control. 'No, it's certainly not that. We've got sacred dance, and there's a choir from Chicago.'

Jan could hear the desperation in his voice. She'd done enough. 'Well, thanks so much for joining us, the Venerable Archdeacon of Wandsworth, James Roberts.' She hit the 'now' button, which started the next track, speaking over the ten seconds of introductory music.

'And as we leave James Roberts to do it his way on millennium night, here's the late great Frank Sinatra doing it "his" way.'

James sat in the chair, his hands still gripping the table, his heart thumping. He felt conned. Embarrassed. Angry. He looked down at his stiff white hands. He'd just endured a white knuckle ride. Hardly the right preparation for divine worship in the Abbey.

On the fourth finger of his left hand was his wedding ring, and on the fourth finger of his right hand a small blue ring on which was painted a delicate yellow Celtic cross. He felt reassured. Helen and Anita would be praying. He glanced at his watch.

He stood and strode confidently to the doorway just in time to see the Precentor raise his hand. James walked towards the choir, tall and straight, determined to present himself as one prepared. With perfect precision the choir began the processional hymn, 'O God our help in ages past'.

The choir stepped solemnly down the centre aisle of the nave followed by the Beadle and the Dean and Chapter. It was a moment to savour. The congregation stood. It seemed as though two thousand years of history were echoing around the sanctuary as they glided forward. James Roberts, as preacher, joined the procession, and behind him followed the religious leaders of the nation.

The line of robes seemed to take an age to wind its way down the length of the cathedral. With each slow step James felt more nervous. He looked up at the tall stone pulpit towering above him and wondered again why he had been chosen to deliver the millennium address in the Abbey.

He had concluded that, as chair of the London millennium arrangements committee, the Bishop had considered him to be the clergyman most aware of the issues involved. Or perhaps he'd been nominated because of his recent MA thesis on Celtic Christianity. Or even because someone, somewhere, had heard that he was a good preacher. He found the honour bestowed on him a disturbing puzzle.

In fact, he had not been chosen because he was chair of the committee, nor for his Celtic thesis, nor even because of his reputation as a preacher. He had been chosen because the Dean and the Bishop couldn't agree on who should do it and his name was their point of compromise.

The Bishop had wanted a black Pentecostal

evangelist and the Dean a Roman Catholic cardinal. James Roberts represented safe middle ground between the two. Unaware of the true reason why he had been chosen to speak to the nation on millennium night, James Roberts clasped his prayerbook tight. Within it were the sermon notes over which he had laboured for many hours.

Perhaps he had been trained for this moment. Those arduous years at theological college with barely five GCSEs to his name. Those long dark nights struggling to learn New Testament Greek. Those endless philosophy lectures, and that mind-numbingly boring theology that he had struggled to read. Perhaps he had been groomed for this moment.

Yet, in his heart of hearts he knew that these things had not prepared him. Something much more recent and something much more mysterious had done that. Something which had lit a fire within him which he knew nothing would ever extinguish. Even as he approached the preacher's throne he knew that Anita was with him in spirit, and that she was praying.

* * *

'My ministry is over. I've got nothing more to give.' He was bent low, holding his hands out to the crackling log fire and seeking some security from its warmth.

'It's good that you feel like that, James,' Sister Anita whispered. She leant forward in her wheelchair and touched him on the shoulder. 'There's hope for you yet.'

He had just completed his research for the MA. His three years of visits to the Celtic Studies Unit at Swansea University and to the Sisters of the Seashore on the Gower had finally come to an end.

'I think I know all that there is to know about Celtic

spirituality, but all it's done is made me feel a failure.' He looked up at her. She had a way of getting him to be real, but it was so unthreatening. He felt so safe.

'If it's made you feel a failure, James, it's just opened the way for you to make a new beginning.' She was gentle and reassuring.

He looked up at her, puzzled, but said nothing. Anita smiled and continued.

'Maidoc felt a failure, you know. It was failure that drove him to Ireland to study at the monastery, and it was failure that drove him out to the cave on Worm's Head to empty his life of everything but the love of Christ. And even there on Middle Worm, completely focused on the disciplines of prayer, he felt a failure. That's where he wrestled with the demons of his past.'

'But how do I do that? How does an archdeacon do that?' He felt trapped by his job, by his role, by his ministry.

'You must endeavour to empty your life of all that's not of Christ. Like Maidoc, you must live an uncluttered life. You must meet your demons, James, and claim Christ's victory over them like Maidoc did. Remember his prayer? "In the Name of Christ, be gone!" You must become one of the people of the Way and learn how to be more open to the leading of the Holy Spirit.'

Anita paused, allowing the words to sink deeply into his soul. 'You, James Roberts, must be the salt of the earth in Wandsworth and the leaven in the lump in the Anglican communion. You must discover God's potential within you. Share in the very energy of Christ's resurrection.'

There, at that humble fireside, Archdeacon James Roberts allowed Sister Anita to pray for him. It was quite the most beautiful prayer he had ever heard, though he couldn't remember a word of it afterwards. What he could remember, however, was an overwhelming sense of the presence of Christ. Jesus was no longer confined to the religious trappings of his Anglican heritage. From that moment onwards Christ infused all things everywhere.

James knelt and made a new profession of faith. It was, for him, the culmination of three years of research. Research which had moved him from a religion of the head to a religion of the heart. For the first time in his life he truly felt the power of Christ's presence.

Sister Anita reached into the pocket of her woollen cardigan. 'I'm not sure if this is really appropriate, but I'd like you to have it anyway.'

She handed him a blue ring, with a yellow Celtic cross painted on it. 'This is the ring of the Sisters of the Seashore. We all wear it as a sign of our belonging completely to Christ. It reminds us to love him with all our being.'

James took the ring and slid it onto the fourth finger of his right hand. He was overwhelmed, without words.

'So now you're officially one of the Sisters of the Seashore!'

Anita's cheerful voice released him.

He smiled. 'Even though I'm a brother and there's no seashore in London?'

'I think God understands.' She beamed.

'Yes, I expect he does.'

* * *

The hymn before the sermon was drawing to a close. James Roberts stood aloft in the towering pulpit and took one last gaze at the assembled congregation before him. The hymn finished and the congregation was seated. He put on his reading glasses and drew a deep breath.

'We stand, tonight, on the verge of a great new beginning. Not only a new year, nor a new century, but a new millennium. Tonight isn't a night for fears and worries, it's a night for hopes and dreams and for asking ourselves — what does God want to do with the world in the new millennium?'

The Dean looked at the Canon Treasurer and raised his eyes. He was rarely impressed by sermons, and he'd already decided that this one was not up to par. The Canon raised his eyes dutifully in humble imitation.

'Well, for a start, I believe he wants to disestablish the Church of England.' The Dean quickly glanced at the pulpit in disbelief. 'Our history of church and state is a long history of institutional incest. The church must be free to become the conscience of the government, not its lap-dog.'

The Canon looked at the Dean as if to ask, shall I stop him? The Dean looked ashen. He was gripping the arms of his ornately carved throne and wincing in disagreement.

'I believe that God wants the denominational barriers demolished. The time of denominations is passed. The time of partnership has come. Let the Salvationists wear their uniforms and the Methodists sing their hymns; let the Baptists immerse their believers and the Catholics preserve the Eucharist. But let us all be known as the Church of England, for that, truly, is what we are.'

The Lieutenant Colonel from the Salvation Army glanced across at the General Secretary of the Baptist Union and smiled a furtive smile. They knew that James Roberts had recently come to believe these things, but they'd never thought he'd say them. Not on millennium eve. Not in the Abbey. Not, especially, in front of the Dean.

'The dawn of a new millennium is the dawn of new hope. We, as Christians, have much to be ashamed of in

55

our history. We have sometimes called for holy war, we have encouraged rape, pillage and massacre in the name of the gospel. We have remained silent against injustice. We have been coerced into supporting wicked rulers and corrupting authorities. We have stood silent in the flood-tide of pornography. We have run away from conflict. We have blood on our hands. So, at the start of a new millennium let's start with ourselves, let's be reconciled as Christian brothers and sisters, that we, in turn, might become the people of reconciliation for our generation.'

The Dean was squirming in his seat. He would be on the phone to the Bishop of Southwark as soon as possible. James Roberts had overstepped the mark, and the Church of England has quiet but firm ways of handling those who don't play the game by the rules.

Helen Roberts looked down at her feet. She'd had no idea that James was going to use this moment, of all moments, to tell the world what had happened to him on the Gower in recent months. She'd seen the change in him — gentle at first but later radical, dramatic and life transforming.

It had started with the MA he was doing at Swansea University, an MA in Celtic Christianity. He had discovered that it had evolved through the interaction of the Christian tradition with many pre-Christian myths and rituals.

The pre-Christian Celts were particularly sensitive to God in the natural world. At the centre of this Celtic type of spirituality was a sense of presence. The Celtic hermits had managed to absorb this but to make it Christian. They were God-intoxicated men and women who sensed God's immanence in every aspect of creation. They felt nurtured and protected by nature, and they loved the wild and beautiful world in which they lived.

James had begun to recognise that he had much to

learn from their reverence for the presence of God in the natural world. It was a kind of spirituality which was intuitive and natural and which sprang directly from the heart.

But these Celtic ideas had not changed the Venerable James Roberts, it was Anita Atwell and Dave Rushden who had done that. In David's heart-driven devotion he had recognised his own failure in spiritual things, and in Anita's prayers he'd begun to sense Christ's presence in everything. For the first time in his life James Roberts had got in touch with himself, his feelings and his God.

James cleared his throat and continued. 'Our experience of sharing the bread of life should provide us with the motivation to tackle the problems of world hunger, poverty and the deteriorating environment. These have reached crisis proportions for everyone on earth. Ultimately, the survival of everyone may depend on whether we reverse the ecological destruction which goes hand in hand with widespread poverty.'

Helen smiled warmly at him. Perhaps, even in that enormous crowd, her smile would be recognised. She had supported him through thick and thin. She would support him though this, too. But she feared the consequences, and she feared his capacity to cope with them.

James turned to the last page of his notes. 'Recently, I have been studying the lives of the Celtic saints. These men and women have contributed much to the development of our Christian heritage here in the British Isles. But one man, particularly, should be remembered here, tonight.

'His name was Maidoc, and for four long years he lived alone on a rocky island off the coast of Wales and prayed. He had witnessed the collapse of an ordered world that had somehow seemed immutable. The ruins of the Roman walls, villas and garrisons were strewn around the countryside. But liberation from the Roman Empire had not bought the paradise on earth which many had been hoping for.

'Famine and disease were still rampant, and invaders still came with every passing year. Maidoc saw so clearly that their strength to face the future lay in belonging to each other in the Celtic church and in the love of the Christ who is the only hope for the world.

'Fifteen hundred years later, we find ourselves in much the same position. Liberated from the oppressive Victorian values and institutions of our forefathers, we find ourselves adrift in a world in which even science is now unable to control its power.

'Maidoc can be an inspiration to us. He can show us a way out of our confusion. The confusion which human intellect divorced from feeling has led us into. He can teach us how to feel God again. He can lead us towards the spiritual rebirth of our nation. The time of materialism is over, the era of mass culture is waning, the age when we thought science could solve all our problems is at an end, the utopian optimism of modernism is finished.

'Let the new millennium signal a new start. A new relationship with God, a new awareness of the Holy Spirit, a new sense of the living Christ in our lives. As we join with countless millions of others, light our candles and recite the Lord's prayer, let us remember that tonight we say goodbye to the past, and tonight we recognise that there is no future outside of Our Father, who art in heaven, whose name is to be hallowed and whose kingdom will surely come.'

He gently closed the prayerbook on his notes, clasped it tight, and turned to make the perilous descent down the pulpit steps to the Beadle standing patiently below, baton in hand. As he turned he glanced across at the Dean who was standing in front of the altar ready to lead the midnight prayers. There was a look he had never seen in the Dean's eyes before: barely contained rage. Somewhere, deep inside, James shivered. He had upset the establishment and, undoubtedly, his future was now in question.

* * *

Global Oil Headquarters. The City of London

Three miles away in the heart of the City of London on millennium night the streets were deserted. The large tower blocks were dark and empty save for the solitary perambulations of the occasional security guard. Here in this heartland of business, New Year's Eve was a time for fun, not for work.

Everywhere, that is, except on the seventeenth floor of Global Oil Networks. For, in the blaze of bright neon ceiling lights, a team of thirty-two people were in a state of high tension.

In six-inch letters at the top of the wall in front of them there was a projected countdown. It counted down in minutes, seconds and milliseconds, informing them that they were 07:00:00 to midnight, Greenwich Mean Time. Tonight was the most difficult situation which Global Oil had ever faced. Tonight they would know if the millennium computer bug would break the system.

The millennium bug had become a living nightmare for many corporate executives. The cost of correcting it in the USA and Europe, estimated at 717 billion dollars, had spiralled out of control. The nearer the deadline came, the more companies had been panicked into spending astronomical sums.

Charles Meddison, a small dark Yorkshireman in

59

Ralph Lauren jeans and Calvin Klein T-shirt, was standing in front of a large electronic display panel beneath the flicking numbers of the countdown. It covered most of the wall in front of the room. It was a world map, and it was pierced by scores of flashing pin-pricks of light. Stretching across vast swathes of the map was a small yellow ribbon of light which linked the flashing white lights into a unified whole.

The pin-pricks were sub-stations, where computers and microprocessors controlled the pump systems. The yellow line represented liquid gold: the national, international and intercontinental oil pipelines. At various points across the map were large red pools of light which showed the status of a major oil refinery or transfer terminal.

When you were running a global operation in which pipelines crossed continents and time-zones it was vital that you all lived by the same clock. The whole system used Greenwich Mean Time, and no matter what time of day it was in Houston, Tokyo, Shetland or Rotterdam, all of the processes at Global Oil Networks ran precisely on GMT.

Each of the scores of computers and microprocessors received an international satellite signal which kept them locked into Greenwich. Generally this worked very well, but on millennium night it had created something of a nightmare. All of the systems in all of the international locations would click from 99 to 00 simultaneously at precisely midnight GMT. Only then would Charles Meddison know if they were all millennium compatible.

'Well, it all seems to be functioning.' Charles was trying to sound confident. 'All we can do now is wait. Any questions?' There was a tense silence. No one was quite sure what was going to happen.

Charles stood surveying the three rows of operators

in front of him. Each was seated behind a VDU. Each was monitoring the flow in one of the company's terminal centres — the flashing lights on the world map — and checking the status of the refineries. They could tell, instantly, whether there was any change in the pressure of oil flowing through their section.

Next he gazed at the three screens before him. Each represented a continent in which the company had interests, and each enabled him to focus in on any one of the scores of control centres which might be causing trouble.

Standing at the back of the room, without a desk or a screen, lounged John Maples from Swindon. His job was 'corporate scenario planning'. As trouble-shooter, he would only be called upon if things got out of hand.

The red light above the central screen on Charles Meddison's desk flashed. He knew that, 4,800 miles away in Houston, the Chief Executive Officer of Global Oil and his two assistants were watching him on the corporate videolink.

'How's it going?' The southern American drawl of the CEO was unmistakeable.

'Fine, sir. The system's all up and running.'

'We gonna make it?'

It was a question which Charles Meddison would rather not answer because he could not.

'I hope so, sir.'

'You'd better deliver a bit more than hope, son. We're all counting on you.' There was a hard edge to the voice.

Charles remembered his first meeting with the CEO. June 1998. A Friday afternoon. Houston like an oven.

'Charles, we've been watching you, and we think you've got potential. As you know we've not been making good progress with this millennium bug fiasco . . . and

61

we figure that you're the best techie we got. You've got eighteen months, unlimited resources — you can crack heads and break balls — but get the job done. Read me?'

There had been a note of urgency, even panic in his voice. A report from Cap Gemini had confirmed that one in six major companies would miss the deadline, and the board had made it clear that if Global Oil Networks was one of them they'd have the CEO for breakfast.

Charles had read him. The words were burnt deep into him. At the tender age of twenty-six he had never expected to get such a project. It could mean a giant leap up the corporate ladder. But it was a huge gamble. If it worked, he'd be made for life. He daren't even ponder the alternative.

It had started off well. He'd drawn up a plan, created a timescale, and put in a budget. It had not been easy, the Board had allocated twenty-four per cent extra to their 1999 information technology budget, but Charles knew that it would take as much again. Scared by the scenario of a major breakdown, they had reluctantly agreed to pay.

Charles estimated that it was possible to change the programme in hundreds of terminals and substations in eighteen months, and he had convinced the CEO that he could do it. But the one factor which he'd never considered at the outset was manpower.

So many companies were panicking over the millennium bug that there wasn't a computer programmer to be hired anywhere in the world. Even the 20,000 programmers specifically trained by the UK government to deal with the fault were not enough. There were just too few skilled people in the field, and those that did have the know-how could charge whatever they wanted. It was a skills shortage of global proportions.

As his plan of changing the programmes in hundreds of computers had slowly but irrevocably slipped behind schedule, one of his staff had come up with a novel idea. They'd employed six teams of US and British science students over the long summer vacation of '99, trained them up, given them manuals and a satellite phone helpline, and despatched them to every corner of the global network to modify the company's ageing computer systems. There was no way of telling whether they had all done the job right. No way, until midnight on millennium eve.

If one of the electronic management systems in a pipeline went down it would prove difficult; if a line of them went down that pipe could be shut for months. But if a major terminal closed when its computers moved from 99 to 00 the implications could be disastrous. Whole oilfields could be jeopardised and the spot market made vulnerable.

This was the most important night of Charles Meddison's career. Everything was riding on it. He had an uneasy feeling that there was something, or someone, he had overlooked.

John Maples sauntered by and peered over the younger man's shoulder. He looked into the camera and the unseen audience in the Global Boardroom. 'Even if the shit does hit the fan, we can manage the crisis. Trust me, you'll end up with a good spot price in Rotterdam, shares high . . . and smelling like roses.' He smiled confidently. It was part of his job to exude that kind of confidence. He planned and delivered the best scenarios in every crisis.

The videolink crackled, and the CEO sighed. 'I hope to God it doesn't come to that.'

As they had rehearsed, each of the operators was taking detailed readings of oil-flow and pounds per square inch. Every aspect of the system had been surveyed and checked as running normally in the thirty minutes previously.

Charles strolled across and stood behind the young woman monitoring the northern sector of the British Isles. Her perfume was familiar, Ysatis. It reminded him of Susan, and the deep ache within him returned. It seemed strange that anything could trigger it. It was something over which he had no control. This loss had been the true cost of the whole enterprise: the loss of his marriage and his kids. He wondered how they were, and what they would be doing that millennium night in Houston.

The ache of that broken relationship lingered around him night and day. Yet he kept busy enough to suppress it. It was strange how, like now, the smallest thing could bring it all back. A wisp of perfume and he could see her face again, and feel the pain.

He looked down at the screen. The operator was reviewing the lists of data which were constantly being updated from the central control room at Sullom Voe in Shetland.

The Ninian pipeline readings flashed onto the screen. They monitored the flow in the 108-mile long pipeline. The two-and-a-half inch thick pipe had a diameter of thirty-six inches and its cathodic protection used zinc anodes undersea and impressed current on the land-line section. Oil pressure had to remain constant throughout.

'What's the reading on Ninian?'

The operator quickly scanned the discharge readings from the three North Sea platforms known as Heather, Alwyn North and Magnus, and then from the gathering platform called Ninian Central. She then checked these against the data from the network of computers within the major Sullom Voe terminal in Shetland.

The operator slid the mouse over a list of options.

'All readings within 300psi's of the test pressure of 2,315 pounds per square inch.'

Charles Meddison stepped back over to his desk and sat down. The projected clock read 4:55:46. From here on he would be completely focused on the three screens in front of him. Any lapse of concentration could cost him everything.

If one of the systems did go down he had to follow defined procedures without emotion or regret. He might have to prioritise any number of possible emergencies so that they were dealt with in strict order of importance. No one could do anything without his authority. At the epicentre of a crisis, only one person can be in charge.

He hoped above hope that it would all work. He had adopted Bob Bemer's radical solution throughout the whole system. It was called Vertex 2000, and expanded dates vertically. Each space reserved for two-digit years contained a minute surplus, and this excess was enough room to piggyback additional information for denoting the century.

Many programmers hated the Vertex system, however, because it used object code, or machine language, a language which humans cannot readily understand. Using Vertex was a big risk . . . but given the extent of the problem at Global Oil, Charles had been left with little choice. If it didn't work, he could say goodbye to all this, the corporate lifestyle, the ladder to the top, and the network of relationships that revolved around the oil business. If it didn't work out right he could kiss goodbye to everything he'd struggled for.

The six-inch numbers projected onto the wall of 'crisis control' clicked to 00:00:00, and there was an intense silence. Charles Meddison, who was not a praying man, came as near to praying as he had ever done.

Each operator was gazing at their screen. The forty

or more readings displayed in front of them were scanned constantly for any change or fluctuation.

John Maples was braced at the back of the room, his earlier nonchalance gone, arms crossed, waiting for disaster. For him, this could be the biggest opportunity of his career and he hoped above hope that the alarms would start to ring.

The milliseconds spun relentlessly on: +5.+7.+10.+14.

Charles looked up at the illuminated world map. None of the flashing white lights had turned red. None of the yellow lines had turned blue. None of the red terminals had started to flash. It was looking good.

He was suddenly aware that he was still holding his breath. Sweat was trickling down his face, and his shirt was stuck to his back. He surveyed the three continental monitors in front of him and the great lines of data scrolling before him which simply registered 'OK'.

He sighed and reflected on how unfeeling computers can be. Here he was, asking the screen if the entire global oil network was about to collapse and all it could say was 'OK'. It was a weird world.

The milliseconds spun on. Charles Meddison stood and watched them. The world had stopped to celebrate two thousand years and yet he still lived in milliseconds. Time was something measured, quantified, priced. He wondered if he would ever get beyond this incessant fixation with it and live at a slower pace. It was a longing which overshadowed him, a longing that disturbed his busy successful days.

Thirty seconds passed, and then the big projected letters showed: +01:00:00. With the first minute behind them, things were looking good. There was still an intensity of silence. No one moved. All the screens continued to flash 'OK'.'OK'.'OK'.

John Maples crept out to the toilet. He lived in tension, but never before in this kind of tension. Another five minutes passed and Charles leant back on his chair. He could sense the strain of the months falling away from him like heavy weights. A wave of light-headed emotion surged through him and he broke into a smile.

He punched the button to Houston where New Year was still hours away. 'We've passed the five-minute marker. All systems showing OK.'

The line crackled back. 'We're not clear yet. Keep focused.'

John Maples crept back into the room and wandered behind the lines of computer operators glancing at each screen. 'OK', 'OK', 'OK'. He was beginning to feel very nauseous.

As the illumined figures showed +11:05:56 the phone rang. It was the red emergency line, and for some seconds no one answered it.

* * *

St Thomas's Hospital. London

Dave was still feeling horribly scared. He lay immobile, with machines hooked up on every side of him and stared out from his cubicle at the clock above the doorway. The doctors and nurses had gone and he was alone with PC Breeson.

'What were you doing in Downing Street tonight? Why did you go there? What were you trying to achieve?' PC Breeson was looking down at him.

Dave looked back blankly.

'Political, was it?' the policeman asked firmly.

'Was I in Downing Street?'

'You sure were, sunshine, up onto those gates like a flaming lunatic.'

'And why did I do that?'

The policeman felt a cold wave of suspicion sweeping over him. 'I was rather hoping that you could tell me.'

Dave closed his eyes. He was ready to sleep.

PC Breeson was getting nowhere. He felt frustrated and bored. Slowly and quietly he crept out of the ward, gently shutting the rubber swing doors behind him. As he strode up the corridor he saw a young doctor approaching him. Despite her white coat and rather boyish haircut, he found her very attractive.

'Tell me, doc. What's the story with this guy?'

She smiled a warm smile, grasped him by the arm, and walked him up the corridor. 'Nasty head injury, but there doesn't seem to be anything life threatening. He'll have to have a CT scan to check for brain damage. But we've really got to work out whether it's a case of antero-grade amnesia or retrograde amnesia.'

'Which means?' Breeson smiled at her. There was a look in her eye which convinced him that she was flirting with him.

'Which means he can't acquire new factual information if it's anterograde, and can't remember events prior to the injury if it's retrograde.'

'But he can talk OK and he seems quite alert.' Breeson was wondering if it was all some complex ploy.

'That's quite usual. The typical amnesiac appears perfectly normal in use of vocabulary, knowledge about the world, and level of intelligence. They just can't pull out the right files from memory. I'm going to see him now. You can take a break if you want.'

Breeson thanked her and ambled on up the corridor. He was following the sound of laughter, and would soon down a glass of rather cheap wine and sing 'Auld Lang's Syne' with a crowd of nurses who'd gathered in the staff-room of Accident and Emergency at St

Thomas's. It wouldn't be much of a celebration, but it was better than nothing.

Dave lay completely still with his eyes shut tight. He was trying to find some inner stillness. Something that he had done many times over the last eight years. That side of his character had grown through the influence of his partner Eva. She had taken him to an 'Open Centre' where people gather to meditate and to seek divine truth. The whole experience had been a revelation to him.

The venue was a seventeenth-century farmhouse. For many years it had been practically derelict but now was nearly renovated. Inside and outside the building there were dozens of young people, some working on the land and others on the rebuilding of the outhouses. There was an atmosphere of intense concentration.

Somewhere in the distance a bell clanged and suddenly there was silence. The people continued to work, but everyone concentrated on a process they called 'self-remembering'. This continued for about ten minutes, and then a second bell called everyone together for meditation.

The discipline of meditation was at the heart of the community's life and they set aside an hour for it each morning, afternoon and night. Eventually this discipline became a part of Dave's everyday life, and the observance of it had made a profound impact on him.

Dr Jennings entered the cubicle and sat silently beside her patient. The second hand of the ward clock swept past midnight and somewhere, in the distance, there was a massive cheer and the clink of glasses. Far along the distant corridors of the hospital people were singing words which Dave no longer recognised.

'Should old acquaintance be forgot . . . .'

Dr Jane Jennings sensed Dave's inner anguish, and she reached over and gently placed her hand on his. In that instant he knew she cared. 'Happy New Year,' she whispered, looking across at him with caring eyes.

'Yes, I guess so.' Dave opened his eyes.

'I'm Doctor Jennings. Jane. I'm going to look after you. OK?'

Dave smiled, and Jane thought it strange that, even when you didn't know who a patient was, you could know instinctively whether you liked them or not. There is a kind of recognition between human beings which surpasses the trivia of name, address and phone number. She sensed that he was intensely spiritual and innately sensitive. She was right.

Dave lay completely still and closed his eyes tight shut. He had never felt so alone in his life nor so confused. Why was his head strapped up in a high collar? What had happened? And, more importantly, who was he?

* * *

Dave's first introduction to deep meditation had taken place in the great barn at the Open Centre. The barn had been adapted to comply with the laws of ancient geometry, a concept long recognised in the East as a science. Echoes of it are still to be seen in many medieval cathedrals in Europe. The building's proportions were designed to awaken a new sense of understanding, and they certainly had the desired effect on him whenever he went there.

During the meditation sessions Dave found that it was easy to be still physically but he always struggled to be still in his emotions and his mind. When at last he achieved it, however, he was amazed to discover that it was a corporate experience shared with all the others. He was so moved by this that the philosophy of silence gradually became the foundation for his whole life.

The silence at the Open Centre prompted him to explore his own interior silence. He began to open his inner ear and to be attuned to the sounds within his inner silence. It was like learning a new language and it took time and patience. There, on millennium night, he had no memory of the barn or the disciplines of the Open Centre but he reached out instinctively for that silence. At midnight in St Thomas's Accident and Emergency Department on millennium night, however, it was nowhere to be found.

* * *

Jane Jennings looked at him. She held his hand and sensed the inner turmoil within. They sat, doctor and patient, man and woman, and for just a moment, experienced some connection.

Although David Rushden did not recognise it there were aspects of his true self that he was yet to face up to. Reflections of his scarred past that he was yet to understand. For him, millennium night was to be the next stage of his perilous journey of self-discovery.

* * *

The Worm

Josh looked around him at his little community, each so different and each so precious. He loved them all, even Jez, who was, perhaps, the hardest to understand. There they were, the seven of them, standing alone on a rocky outcrop and linked mysteriously to those unknown generations who had stood there before them. He turned and looked out beyond the Worm to the timeless distant horizons of sea and sky.

In his mind's eye he saw the Celtic pagans, standing in the firelight beside them. They were burning offerings in worship of their great Welsh god Govannon. He was the divine smith and the god of all metalwork, and fire was the way to appease him. Those Celts loved Govannon because they were outstanding metalworkers and all the important symbols of their culture were forged in metal. Josh smiled. How ironic that, just around the next bay lay the vast furnaces of Port Talbot steelworks. Perhaps Govannon had moved on to steel!

Josh looked around him at his friends. They were all silent, linked by some unseen force to the past. On millennium night Josh Lake recognised his transience and, unknowingly, began to reach out for something permanent.

Josh, the public-school boy from Winchester, had adopted a Celtic culture and made it his own. He was, perhaps, more Welsh than many who lived in the principality. He believed above all that a culture rested on something more than language. A culture was something imbibed, drawn into the soul, and lived from day to passing day.

Here on Worm's Head his Celtic heroes had gathered to taste the sweet wine of victory. Here on Worm's Head they had celebrated their rituals and paid their dues with the spoils of war. This was the grassy slope where they knelt and thanked the gods who favoured them. This was the place where they had thrown their fine metalwork of war into the water as a thank offering. Swords, spears, shields, chariot and harness fittings, ironworkers' tools, trumpets, cauldrons and slave chains. All thrown into the murky deep to say thanks to the supernatural. Sometimes they had even sunk their boats beside the Worm as a tribute to the mercy of the gods of war.

But there was another chapter in the Celtic history of the Worm, a phase that Josh had chosen to ignore. For Maidoc, too, had lain silent on this spot and gazed up at the canopy of stars above. Here he'd sat and watched the sea and wept for the loss of his young wife, long dead in childbirth. Here he relived her last questioning look, the look that cracked his heart.

And there that night, millennium night, beyond the veil of Josh Lake's simple human understanding, Maidoc lifted the hem of eternity to glimpse him there and pray for him again.

Josh gathered his little community around him. It was approaching midnight, and as on many important occasions before, he had an ancient Celtic story to tell.

'Tonight is the story of Limpet Rock. It's about a man named John and a rocky outcrop cut off by the tide, just like this one.

'When he was sixteen his mother and father and his elder brother all died in their boat as they tried to ride out a great storm. John Fowler was left all alone.

'So he built a cottage beside the sea, and he was a very lonely man. Most of his days he was out fishing in the bay, but he fished all alone. He rarely saw anyone, for he lived in such a desolate place. And he felt very, very lonely.'

Josh glanced across at Jez, who was puffing streams of smoke from his new cigarette and looking out to sea. Jez was a loner, just like John Fowler.

'Well, one misty day he looked out to the rock and thought he saw six or seven shadowy figures there. So he decided to go out to find them, but after he scrambled across the rocks all he could find was a seal skin near a still small pool.

'He took the skin home and hid it behind his fireplace, and then went back to the rock to wait and see what would happen. As he sat looking out to sea in that place just like this, a beautiful woman emerged from the still waters and sat beside him.

'Tell me sir, have you found a seal skin?'

'It must have been washed away by the tide,' he replied, hoping she wouldn't know that he lied.

Josh looked around at the faces of his little community. They were spellbound by a story which resonated with their own lives in different ways.

The beautiful woman stayed and lived with John Fowler, and they were very happy. And they had two children, a boy and a girl. John never mentioned the seal skin, for he believed that some kind of bargain with the sea had been made. The sea had taken one family away and had repaid him with another.

One day, after a terrible gale, John Fowler had to repair the chimney of their home. And as he was on the roof his son was moving the chimney bricks below when he found the folded skin. He threw it to his sister and she went running to her mother to show her the soft beautiful fur.

The mother hugged the fur close to herself and then she took the children, each in turn, and hugged them close as well. And then she slowly walked across to Limpet Rock.'

It was nearly midnight though Josh wasn't aware of it. He never carried a watch and resented everyone's preoccupation with time. Time was best measured by the tides, tides that flowed in and flowed out, tides controlled by nature not by humankind. The story continued.

'John Fowler looked across from his roof-top and saw his beautiful wife edging her way to the rocks. He climbed down the ladder and raced after her. Gasping and panting, he approached the rock and there he saw her. Those big brown eyes were gazing at him as she slithered away into the deep.

'For years afterwards he looked out to sea and hoped she would return, but finally he recognised that that last look is the look that cracks the heart. The look of farewell.'

It was like a sermon, but not preached by a priest and not from a pulpit. Josh, with Pol in his arms, had mesmerised the whole community with the story of Limpet Rock and, as the story finished, they all sat in hushed silence and gazed out beyond the rocky outcrop to the distant dark horizon beyond.

'And the story of Limpet Rock is for us. Relationships come, relationships go, but relationships are what, ultimately, it's all about.'

Jez breathed another long stream of smoke out into the chill air, and it dissipated invisibly across the vast ocean all around them. Jez did not like the story of Limpet Rock for he didn't really like relationships. He lay back and looked up at the stars. Time was dragging by and he wished he'd gone into Swansea to join the party.

It was midnight on the Worm, though they didn't know it. No one had a watch but it didn't really matter. For all of them except Jez the whole night had been a celebration, a marker, a new turning point for the world.

Jez lay on his back, with wisps of smoke rising above him. Pol went and lay beside him. One by one the others joined them until they were all lying on their backs looking up at the stars.

No one spoke. Even Jem had stopped her whining. They were silent in the presence of the great vastness of space, of the slow turn of the planet, of the faint wisps of cloud flying past and of the strong sure pounding of the ocean on the rocks below.

They were in a cathedral more spectacular than Westminster Abbey; a holy place where words seemed strangely unimportant. And watching them from beyond the edge of eternity was Maidoc, who long ago had stepped out of the restrictions of time to live in the endless expanse of heaven.

* * *

Rhosili village

Anita Atwell looked out at the long twisting shape of Worm's Head which was so dark and foreboding against the moonlit sky. The flickering bonfire was clearly visible on the far edge of the cliffs. Her mind went back to the history of the rocky outcrop and the great fire built there by the Irish invaders in December 499, celebrating victory at their conquest of the region.

The Irish had invaded the south-west of Wales in great numbers that year. They came from the dynasty of Leinster, and arrived by ship to land on the beaches at Rhosili, Horton and Port Eynon. The long expanses of sand were ideal for beaching their boats and the sparsely populated Gower Peninsula meant that they could prepare at leisure for their sorties deeper into Wales.

They came in sufficient numbers to establish a kingdom of their own, and to implant the Irish language and their Christian Celtic culture. It was from this stronghold that they would set out on their voyage to Cornwall, where they would establish a cultural movement which would dominate the region for more than four centuries.

They brought with them a form of Christianity which focused on the monastery. Different monasteries modelled the emphases of their individual founders, and these communities of prayer soon became the dominant religious force in the land.

Some of these early Irish invaders settled permanently in the peninsula and established a community at Llangennith. The Celtic root word Llan came to mean 'enclosed land', and soon 'an enclosed cemetery', then 'the area of land served by the church'. Over the centuries that followed it became known as 'the township surrounding a parish church', and later still a common noun simply meaning 'church'.

Maidoc had been greatly influenced by them, and in the sorrow of his personal tragedy, the loss of his young wife in childbirth, they had prayed for him and shown him hope. It was the Llangennith community which had loved him, comforted him, and taught him — and finally sent him to Ireland to study. It was the small praying community at Llangennith which had welcomed him back, and which had recognised his lonely hermit ministry of prayer on the Worm.

Anita loved the shape and form of Celtic Christianity. She had discovered that it spoke to her in ways that institutional religion never could. It was a faith which resonated within her and which gave her the strength to go on.

She looked at the bright blue pot on the coffee table by the veranda widow. It was coated with wax from the candle which was firmly stuck to its lid. At the front of the ceramic pot David had glazed a bright yellow Celtic cross. She reached over and picked it up. How she loved that simple ornament which Dave Rushden had made from some rough clay he'd found beyond Llandimor.

It had been his birthday present to her in mid-November. A gift which she had treasured not for what it was, but for what it represented. It only seemed like yesterday.

* * *

77

'It's for you Anita, for your birthday.' David smiled, pulling the brown paper parcel from his large bright shoulder bag. He handed over the present, brushed back his great mane of dark hair, and sat on the stool to watch.

She opened it slowly, not ripping the paper, but rather peeling it away. She would keep the paper for future use. Even simple actions like this were difficult, and her wrists were throbbing with pain. At last the pot was revealed. She held it out in front of her and beamed.

'Like it?' David never felt secure about giving presents. He'd never been much good at getting the right thing.

'I love it, David, thanks.' Anita struggled slowly up and placed it on the coffee table by the veranda window. 'It will have the place of honour.'

'But why the Celtic cross, David? I thought you had rejected all that?' When Anita Atwell looked you in the eye you couldn't pretend. Her innocence always drew out the truth.

'I never had any contact with the Church, except through you. It always seemed to me an ancient institution worthy of respect. But I never saw any connection between it and my journey.' He looked down at the crackling logs in the fireplace. He loved the smell of wood smoke.

'So is there a connection?' Anita asked hopefully.

'Yes. You're the connection. You are so totally unorthodox and you're on my frequency. You can see. Can't you?'

'I can see, yes.'

'But there are many who call themselves religious who cannot see?' He raked the fire with the poker, stirring the flames again.

'Yes, but I suppose it always was that way. Jesus said, "You have eyes and you see not, ears and you hear

78

not, neither do you understand."' Anita's voice was breaking with emotion.

'I want to see.' He was barely audible.

'You have your spiritual disciplines, don't you?' Her eyes sparkled.

'Yes.'

'And you keep them?'

'Yes.'

'And somehow you're still unfulfilled?'

'Yes.'

'Then perhaps you need to learn from Maidoc. To empty your life of all that fills it and to fill it full with Christ.'

'And how does someone on the edge like me begin?' he asked, uncertainly.

'You can begin at the beginning.' She shuffled uneasily in her wheelchair.

'Go to church, you mean?' He looked puzzled.

'No. Try something they have done in the Orthodox churches of the East for centuries. Simply say, "Lord Jesus Christ, Son of God, have mercy upon me, a sinner."'

'A kind of mantra?'

'Yes. First the whole sentence, with complete concentration, and gradually, as awareness becomes centred on the heart, reduce the words until at last "Lord Jesus" is repeated over and over again.'

'Is that it?'

'That's just the beginning. When you've left all the words behind, your consciousness will be focused within the still centre of your heart. Then you can move from a devotion to Jesus to the indwelling Christ.'

He felt uncomfortable. 'So you like the present, then? I made it myself. I glazed the cross at the Art Centre in the Uni. at Swansea. They've got a kiln there. I wanted it to be right for you.' He was almost child-like in his search for approval.

'I love it, Dave. I really love it. And I'll treasure it for ever.'

'Good.'

'And Dave?'

He looked up at her with trusting eyes. 'Thanks for what you've given me.'

'The present, you mean?'

'No. The understanding. The knowledge. My faith used to be so narrow. But you've taught me that it should embrace the whole of life. As I've travelled this path with you I've seen so much more. I've seen people in their true essence and seen the reality behind all of life. I've been learning from you, Dave.'

'But I'm only a beginner. I don't know anything.' Dave Rushden often felt like that.

'You've taught me that the force which holds everything together is not an impersonal energy, it's love. The love of Christ.'

'But I'm not a Christian.' He poked the fire again.

'Not yet.' She smiled. She reached over to the coffee table, and picked up a small silver Celtic cross lying there. It had been given to her by Mother Superior when she first became a novitiate. Slowly and painfully she stretched her hand towards him. 'Take it. It's yours. To be a reminder along the way.'

In some strange unorthodox kind of way, Dave Rushden became, in that moment, a kind of novice.

* * *

Anita placed the blue pot back on the coffee table beside the veranda window and looked out towards the bonfire on the far horizon. There had been many bonfires on

Worm's Head. Now Josh had lit a bonfire to mark a new millennium. But for her, his bonfire on Worm's Head was burning to the glory of God.

It looked back to the arrival of Celtic Christianity in Wales, and to the life of prayer which Maidoc had so faithfully lived on the Worm. It looked forwards with hope to the rebirth of Christian spirituality and to the arrival of a new generation of men and women of prayer.

The flickering flames of the bonfire were a symbol. The torch of Christianity had been lit afresh for a new millennium that night. Passed from Maidoc to a new generation. And she believed that Dave Rushden would be the man to carry it. How she had prayed for him, and cared for him and, yes, in her own best way had truly loved him.

Dave Rushden was a spiritual man. More spiritual than many she had met in the Church and, perhaps, more honest too. His search for ultimate reality was taking him on a painful journey through his past and bringing him to a fuller recognition of who he was and who he must become. If the Sisters of the Seashore had given her a structure for her prayer, Dave Rushden had given her the heart for it.

Anita had come to understand that in the Western Church there has been a long tradition of contemplative religious orders, both in the Roman Catholic and Anglican churches. But she gradually came to recognise that those contemplative communities had in practice followed reflective meditation, a form which is primarily an intellectual activity.

Not since Maidoc, and the early Celtic saints, had there been a pattern of devotion so rooted in the heart. Dave Rushden had helped her recognise that her own dearth of devotion was caused by this. An inability to connect her emotion to her prayers of praise, her intuition to her intercession. An inability to pray in language too deep for words. Dave Rushden had shown her that Maidoc was right. The deepest forms of prayer demand an awakening of the heart.

Mother Superior had told her to be careful in exploring this. She explained that for centuries the Church has demonstrated a deep reluctance to understand the faculty through which such contemplation occurs. The disappearance of such knowledge was driven by an institutional fear of gnosticism or claims to special knowledge.

Anita knew that Dave Rushden practised this devotion of the heart. All that he had to do now was to focus that discipline on Christ. If Dave Rushden became a Christian he would bring to the Church the knowledge and experience which would make him the Maidoc for the new millennium.

Anita leant back in her wheelchair and sighed. It had all been such a struggle for her, this transformation from teacher to intercessor. From a life lived in the intellect to a life lived in the heart. Tonight, of all nights, she didn't want to be alone. But there was no one else to share it with. The community was at the bonfire and Dave Rushden was away. She looked at the blue pot again and prayed for him. He was hurting so much when he left for London.

* * *

'Eva's gone.' David had whispered, just before he'd left for the Downing Street demo in London.

'When?'

'Three months ago. She says it's over.'

The lifestyle of the New Age community is one of many lovers, many partners. Yet, what many may consider is just a life of sordid immorality, of lust and transient relationships, is in fact a life of pain and loss.

He slowly pulled the photograph of him and Eva from his shoulder bag and handed it to Anita.

'She is a beautiful girl.' Anita smiled and understood. She had known love herself a lifetime ago.

'When she was here it was all so real, but now . . . .' He shrugged his shoulders as if in despair.

'Are you hurting?' Anita said, tenderly.

'Agony. Real agony.' He brushed a tear from his eye.

'I know,' she said. And she did know. She did understand.

'Will it get better? Will I get over it?'

Anita smiled warmly. 'No, you'll never get over it. But you'll learn how to live with it.'

'With the pain, you mean?'

'Yes. With the pain, Dave. It never goes away. Not completely. And it only takes a memory to bring it back.'

'You understand, don't you?' His eyes were almost pleading.

'I've been there, Dave. And, in a real way, I still am there.'

'How do you survive?'

'Through Christ. Who strengthens me.' This was no easy platitude. He was the means of her survival.

* * *

It was eighteen months since Anita had said her final farewells to London life, her career in teaching, and to any hope of a full recovery. In the painful time since arriving in Rhosili she felt that she had lost touch with many important relationships. She was surprised how little she heard from her old friends in London — but they were all so busy.

She pulled herself together, Jesus would not approve of such self-centredness, especially not on this night. She willed herself to put the past behind her and to mark the moment of the turning of a new millennium.

She took the blue pot from the coffee table and looked at the rippling patterns of wax which ran from the candle's stem and down across the Celtic cross. She slowly lit it with a match and placed the pot back on the coffee table. She watched its flickering reflection on the veranda window and gazed out to the moon beyond.

She said the words that were so familiar, yet always so real. The words of the fifth-century Celtic saint called Patrick. Words which his followers had spoken on Worm's Head so many centuries before when they celebrated the arrival of Christianity in this pagan land.

'I bind myself today to the virtue of heaven,
In light of sun,
In brightness of snow,
In splendour of fire,
In speed of lightning,
In swiftness of wind,
In depth of sea,
In stability of earth,
In compactness of rock.

I bind myself today to God's virtue to pilot me,
God's might to uphold me,
God's wisdom to guide me,
God's eye to look before me,
God's ear to hear me,
God's word to speak for me,
God's way to lie before me,
God's shield to protect me,
God's host to secure me,

Against snares of demons,
Against seductions of vices,
Against lusts of nature,
Against every one who wishes ill to me,
Afar and near,
Alone . . . and in a multitude.

Sitting in her tiny cottage overlooking Rhosili Bay, Anita Atwell watched the flickering candle as she prayed. They were words which she'd prayed again and again over recent months. Words which Maidoc would have prayed so many years before. Words which carried her through the long days and even longer nights. Words which sustained her in her darkest hours.

CHAPTER 3
A New Day

Westminster Abbey. London

James and Helen Roberts were the last to arrive at the Dean's cheese and wine party after the service. James had started walking to the car, but Helen, wise and diplomatic in every situation, had stood, arms crossed, beside the rather dirty Ford Mondeo and refused to give him the keys.

'James,' she'd said, in her strongest possible tone, 'all those leaders came tonight because you invited them. The least you can do is to go and wish them a happy new year.'

He looked across at her. He was still clutching his new cassock which was draped over his arm. He loved her, even when she was right. She opened the tailgate and he dropped his robes onto the shelf in a heap, and they walked half-heartedly back towards Dean's Yard.

'Did I do all right tonight?' he asked nervously. He was dreading the Dean's acerbic comments.

'Yes, James. It was fine. A bit "on the edge" perhaps, but it was fine.'

He already felt better. Helen's reassurance meant more to him than anything. Though he knew from the tone in her voice that she had been shocked.

'Helen?' He stopped and turned to face her.

'What?'

'Thanks. Thanks for standing with me, even when you don't fully understand.'

She leant over and kissed him gently on the cheek. 'Oh, I understand all right. You lost your faith, and now you're getting it back. But this time, it's different. Richer. Deeper. Quieter. You've lost the frothy bits. But I think you've found something better.'

'I've found Jesus. Not just in songs and services but in everything and, best of all, in me.'

'I'm doing my best to catch up, James.' Her eyes caressed him.

Roberts grinned broadly. 'I think that all these years I've been trying to catch up with you.'.

Once in the Dean's reception room, James and Helen Roberts stood in the corner, drinks and 'light bites' in hand. They surveyed the scene. Small talk always dominates functions such as these, and there was a happy drone of chatter about the latest ecclesiastical intrigues.

One of the Pentecostal leaders spotted James the moment that he walked in the door. Helen melted into the background.

'Mr Roberts?' The dumpy little Geordie planted himself firmly in James's path.

'Yes?'

'I was deeply disturbed by your sermon tonight. It was pure New Age heresy. It's the instrument that Satan will use to catapult his Antichrist to power. Once he is firmly entrenched he will unite all cults and religions into one. And when Christians refuse to be initiated into this satanic religious system, they will be dealt with very harshly, Mr Roberts.'

'Oh . . . yes . . . ?' James didn't want to upset the man. 'But don't you think we might be able to learn something from them?'

James thought of Dave Rushden, the New Ager who had taught him so much. How different he was from this pompous little man. How normal. How spiritual. How real.

'No,' the Geordie continued impatiently, 'they have nothing to teach us. They are all agents of the devil.'

'My friends aren't agents of the devil, they are fellow travellers on the journey. They're just searching for the truth.'

James pictured David Rushden in this setting. His long black mane of hair, his old army trousers, his creased T-shirt and his colourful shoulder bag. The Dean would have him thrown out. Yet Dave Rushden was as much a spiritual leader as many of those gathered here, perhaps more so.

He owed a debt to Dave Rushden that he could never repay. Dave Rushden had helped him to see that in his endless round of religious duties he had somehow lost his sense of God. He could no longer be still. Dave Rushden wasn't a Christian . . . but his life was an awesome challenge to the barren form of Christianity which James had recently been living.

'My New Age friends have brought me back to God,' James said uncompromisingly.

The little man's eyes bulged and he stared at James as if he had just landed from another planet. 'I will pray for your salvation, Mr Roberts.' He turned and burrowed his way back into the crowd.

The Dean was at the centre of the gathering. He always enjoyed an audience. He was telling some rather embellished story about the last Maundy service, when the Maundy money had gone missing just before the Royals arrived. He had an Imam on his left and a Methodist dignitary on his right. Other religious leaders were gathered in a semi-circle and they were laughing encouragingly.

James Roberts detested receptions. He never knew what to do with the drink in one hand and the plate in the other, and he never knew what to say. There wasn't a coffee table to be seen, and he felt he needed a third hand to manage glass, plate and finger food.

Gradually James and Helen made their way to the edge of the Dean's audience, and tried to look affirming, hoping that some inclusive comment might be thrown their way to bring them into the conversation. None was forthcoming. Helen began to think that perhaps, after all, they might have been wise to have gone straight home.

The Dean moved on to another story about his latest experiences on Radio 4's *Thought for the Day*, and James desperately looked for a way of escape. There was a gentle tap on his arm. 'Mr Roberts?'

He turned to face a diminutive nun, complete with black habit and wimple. She had sparkling blue eyes which seemed, even in this difficult setting, full of fun.

'Yes?' James smiled. This could be a welcome distraction.

'Could I have a word?' She beckoned, James and Helen followed, eagerly looking for a way out of the Dean's irritating patter.

The little nun was stooped and very thin, yet she moved with a jaunty stride over to the Steinway grand piano at the far end of the room. She popped her glass of tomato juice and her slither of quiche onto the shiny black surface. James promptly did the same. Helen looked disapprovingly on. She was sure that to do such a thing was very bad etiquette.

'I'm the Mother Superior of the Sisters of Mercy,' she said in a vaguely Irish accent, 'and I was interested in what you were saying about Celtic spirituality.' She beamed up at him with her clear old eyes.

'And did I get it right?'

'I think, Mr Roberts, that you are the man for the hour.'

'I am?' James Roberts was lost for words.

The little nun smiled and continued, softly, above the hub-hub of polite chatter.

'Where did you find Christ?' She asked, her eyes glistening with curiosity.

'In the Gower. The Sisters of the Seashore.'

The little nun smiled approvingly. 'I'm pleased for you.'

'The religion of the heart. I studied Maidoc, and the more I got to know him, the more I sensed that we have lost that intuitive kind of devotion which was the hallmark of the Celtic saints.' He was almost whispering with embarrassment. The Dean would never understand. 'That's what I discovered.'

'Ah yes. The religion of the heart. And who was your spiritual director?'

'A lady called Anita from the Sisters of the Seashore, and some New Age travellers who seemed to understand.'

'Oh yes. The Sisters of the Seashore. What a remarkable group they are! The hermits of the New Age.'

James continued excitedly. 'She cultivated in me a kind of knowing. An awareness. She taught me to look beyond the visible creation to an even greater reality.'

'Ah yes. St Paul's great cosmic vision in his letter to the Ephesians. When everything in heaven and earth is to be brought into a unity.' Her Irish brogue was growing stronger.

'And the travellers taught me that we're all responsible for transforming creation and for redeeming it.' He was trying to hold himself back, these discoveries had affected him to the very core of his being. He wondered if she might think him a heretic, but he sensed she somehow understood.

'Yes, we're all responsible for bringing it into the

redeeming love of Christ through his death and resurrection.' The nun smiled. She knew the same excitement, and she, too, was having to hold herself back. She whispered,

'I see his blood upon the rose
And in the stars the glory of his eyes,
His body gleams amid eternal snows,
His tears fall from the skies.

I see his face in every flower;
The thunder and singing of the birds
Are but his voice — and carven by his power;
Rocks are his written words.

All pathways by his feet are worn,
His strong heart stirs the ever-beating sea,
His crown of thorns is twined in every thorn,
His cross is every tree.[1]'

James Roberts opened his arms and embraced her. He knew that they had both travelled the same journey. Helen smiled, perhaps it was right that James had gone to the reception, after all.

* * *

Global Oil Headquarters. The City of London

The red emergency phone continued to ring, but Charles remained fixed on the three screens before him.

'Will you get that, John?' he snapped. He must continue to monitor every reading for another nineteen minutes before he could begin to relax.

'He's tied up right now. Who is this? What do you want?'

John Maples was standing in front of the world map, phone in hand, and he broke into a smile, it was good news for him.

'Yes. Yes. I'll tell him.'

'Are you sure? Hold on. Hold on. I'll get him.'

Charles Meddison stared at John Maples. One-sided phone conversations always infuriated him. 'So?'

'It's the shift manager at Baglan Bay in South Wales. The refinery's down. He hasn't got a clue what's going on, or what to do.'

Charles pushed back his chair and moved to the phone. 'When did this happen? Five past twelve?' He sounded incredulous.

There was a long pause, and then Charles simply muttered, 'Oh God.'

He glanced up at the map. The light for Baglan Bay was now flashing bright red. But the refinery hadn't gone down at midnight. What was going wrong?

'Do nothing. Absolutely nothing. I'll come at once. And, by the way, you'd better evacuate the whole area. Understood?'

Charles pressed the intercom button on his desk and stared at the camera into the unseen eyes of the CEO. But before he could speak the red light in front of him clicked on.

'I warned you, Charles, it was all your responsibility,' said the CEO. 'You're the techie. Go get it sorted, as far as we're concerned Baglan is crucial.'

Charles Meddison slumped back in his chair. He had a lot to say, but now wasn't the moment. 'It will be sorted, sir.' Or it's my ass, he thought silently.

Maples phoned the crew on the company jet who were standing by at City Airport. The Lear Jet was in a line with other company planes which had ferried their CEOs to London-based millennial celebrations. The crew was ready to fly Charles Meddison and John Maples anywhere. The Saudi, Egypt, Texas, Kuwait, Poland, Russia, Rotterdam, Shetland or Grangemouth. Anywhere practically, except Baglan Bay.

Charles Meddison snatched up the black flight case which contained an array of computer chips in vacuum-sealed plastic covers, a pile of thick instruction manuals, a list of codes written in longhand in an old exercise book and a small tool kit. He grabbed his brown leather jacket and summoned John Maples to follow him but didn't even say farewell to the rest of his team. He was too preoccupied. What had gone wrong at Baglan?

The two of them stood on the pavement in front of the tall city skyscraper in which they'd been working. John Maples was pulling on his black overcoat to keep out the cold while Charles was looking for a black cab.

'Charles,' smiled John Maples wistfully, 'don't you think you're being a teeny bit optimistic, looking for a cab in the City at 12.15 on millennium night?'

The City was completely deserted. John Maples took out his mobile, called his Freepages number and was instantly connected to Citycab, London's largest computer cab company.

'Yes?' a weary sounding Asian voice replied.

'A cab from The City to City Airport, please.'

'Very sorry, sir. All available cabs are committed for the next hour.'

'You what?'

'Terribly sorry. Call back later.'

'Can we book one?'

'No, sir, not tonight. It's just impossible tonight.' And the phone clicked. He'd been cut off.

No one could describe the chaos at London's largest computer cab company. With only twenty per cent of the normal fleet working that night, and the highest demand of the year, there just weren't enough cabs to go round. Besides, the computer they used to log bookings was down. At precisely midnight it no longer knew which century to book cabs for.

'There's only one thing for it,' sighed Maples.

'And that is?' Charles Meddison yawned. He hated London almost as much as he hated Houston. Yorkshire was his kind of place.

'We'll have to take the Docklands train.'

'Train?' Charles looked in disbelief.

'And tonight there's one big advantage.'

'Which is?'

'Tonight is the only night in the year when Docklands Light Railway is free! Follow me.'

John Maples knew the City intimately, and he strode out across the empty street and made his way into the network of cobbled alleyways and courtyards that have not changed in centuries. Charles Meddison, flight case in hand, struggled to keep up with him.

If you knew where to look you could step back across the centuries and walk in the footsteps of those who knew a different London. Their paces echoed down Oven Lane, across Fish Court and past the old warehouses of London Docks which have taken on a new role as exclusive city offices. These were the alleys that William Shakespeare strolled down on his way to rehearsals at the Globe Theatre. This was where Sir Christopher Wren walked to look at progress on St Paul's Cathedral. John Wesley hurried down these streets on his way to a meeting in Aldersgate Street.

They turned a corner and into St Katharine's Dock. Unlike the surrounding alleyways it was packed with spectators. The old dock has been transformed into a glittering new marina. It was ablaze with light. Twinkling lights from the millionaire cruisers and the huge lumbering Thames sailing barges now used for exclusive dining. Lights from the bevy of dockside restaurants and the yacht club, lights from the dominating Tower Hotel, and just beyond, the lights of Tower Bridge.

They pushed their way past the dense crowd of giddy spectators standing outside Chez Nico's. There was a buzz of excited conversation and white-aproned waiters were pushing through the throng holding high their trays of glasses. The wine was flowing freely on millennium night. Everyone was looking up towards Tower Bridge, waiting for the fireworks to begin.

Suddenly, for the first time in months, Charles Meddison was aware of a life beyond the millennium bug. It felt like he was waking up after a long dream. He pushed his way through the trendy crowd in a desperate attempt to keep up with John Maples who was elbowing his way forwards. Charles suddenly felt very angry.

'John,' he said, urgently.

Maples stopped, turned round and looked him in the eye.

'You ever feel like you missed the party?'

Maples blinked. 'What?'

'We've not even toasted the new year.'

Maples smiled. 'Perhaps it's time we got a life!'

Meddison had once had a life, but he had sacrificed it, freely. He'd offered it up in exchange for a hike up the ladder of promotion. They struggled on through the crowd to Tower Gateway Station and took the London Docklands Light Railway to Silvertown and City Airport.

Within fifteen minutes they had boarded the company's Lear jet emblazoned with the green logo of Global Oil Networks and the crew had prepared for take-off. It roared up the small runway and banked steeply over the River Thames heading east. As it rose to 25,000 feet John

Maples and Charles Meddison sat alone in the eight-seat compartment.

It was certainly luxurious: thick pile carpeting, large leather armchairs and a beautifully illuminated cocktail bar which occupied a third of the cabin. Charles looked out of the window, and as the plane ascended he looked down over the sprawling lights of London.

'Look at that awful monstrosity.' He pointed out of the window.

John Maples clicked off his seatbelt and stretched over to look. 'My dear chap that's not a monstrosity, that's our nation's great tribute to the attributes of body, mind and spirit. And, see where all those lights are?'

Charles Meddison grunted.

'That's Greenwich. The Greenwich Meridian. The Prime Minister's declaring the new millennium officially open. And that's the spot on the planet where your precious computers are focused.'

'Seems strange that I've been thinking about nothing but Greenwich Mean Time for two years but I've never been near the place.'

John Maples smiled. 'Me neither, and I'm a Londoner!'

As the plane reached its cruising altitude it slowly banked round in a wide arc over Essex, and turned to follow the course of the River Thames travelling west. All over the vast metropolis there were sporadic bursts of colour reaching up towards them as they flew overhead. Fireworks for a new millennium.

The Lear swept gently over Windsor at its cruising altitude of 20,000 feet and the auto-pilot was locked onto a westerly course. The Finnish pilot and co-pilot, both trained in their country's air force, had been contracted because the Lear jet operated out of Helsinki.

The crew served the European network of Global

Oil's operations, the centre of which was in Rotterdam. Increasingly, however, the Lear was used to fly international executives throughout Russia. Houston considered rail, road and air travel within Russia substandard, and used the Lear jet for all of their site visits across the former Soviet states. Helsinki was a useful hub for connecting with commercial flights to the Far East and the United States.

Usually a flight attendant travelled with the crew to ply their passengers with drinks and snacks, but on millennium night no one was keen to work no matter what inducements were offered.

The cabin curtain swept open and the young co-pilot beamed. 'Good news. Your guys from the control centre phoned to say they have a clear on everything except Baglan Bay.'

Charles smiled. 'That is good news.'

'You guys sure you want to go to Baglan Bay?' the co-pilot asked.

'Yep.' said Charles, confidently. 'Why? What's the problem?'

'Oh, no problem, except the nearest airport's over twenty miles away. If you can call it an airport, that is.'

Charles looked at John Maples. 'Too late to change our minds?'

'Yep.' Maples smiled. Rather enjoying the ride.

'I've phoned the airport. He's standing by,' smiled the co-pilot.

'He?' Charles looked bemused.

'It's owned by some old chap who collects vintage aircraft. There was one commercial flight there a couple of years ago linking Swansea with Guernsey. But it went bankrupt.'

Swansea airport, converted from an old RAF wartime base, had never been commercially viable. Cardiff, some forty miles east, had scooped all the international traffic. Perhaps it hadn't helped that Swansea airport was situated in the midst of a small peninsula which is nineteen miles long and three to eight miles wide. This peninsula has been declared a Heritage Coast and has been administered under the National Parks and Access to the Countryside Act since 1949.

'Is it safe?' Charles didn't know much about aviation.

'This baby will land anywhere. All the old guy's got to do is turn on the lights, give us clearance, and show us where the gas station is.' The co-pilot smiled again. 'I hope you guys don't mind, but we'll just be dropping you off. We're going home. We might even catch the end of the party.'

'That reminds me.' John Maples looked pleadingly. 'Where are the drinks?'

The co-pilot pointed to the bar. 'It's not locked. Help yourself, gentlemen.'

Charles Meddison and John Maples opened a large bottle of Glenfiddich whisky. Seated side by side in the luxury armchairs of the Lear jet they toasted their health and happiness in the new millennium. Charles felt relaxed for the first time in months, he felt that by and large he had beaten the millennium bug, and therefore had something significant to celebrate.

'Tell me John, what do you actually do? What is scenario planning exactly?'

John Maples never missed an opportunity to sell his services. After all, Charles Meddison could be big in the oil business one day.

'I specialise in thinking ahead.'

Charles Meddison smiled sceptically. 'Don't we all?'

'Believe me, almost no one does. Heard talk of the energy crisis of the seventies? Everyone in the oil industry was basing their plans on simple projections of the status quo.'

'Cheap and plentiful oil supplies,' Charles muttered, to show he understood.

'Everyone, that is, except Royal Dutch Shell. Pierre Wack, my hero, actively considered and mentally rehearsed a set of possible alternative futures. Including the possibility of an OPEC cartel price increase.'

'And?' Charles looked puzzled.

'When the unthinkable actually happened, Shell had made progress on techniques for efficiently converting its oil supply into lighter, more valuable gasoline. And bingo. The rest, as they say, is history.'

'And the millennium bug?' Charles wondered what scenarios John had prepared.

'While you've been chasing round the world replacing chips I've been sitting in my office thinking. Planning the scenarios of everything from total system collapse to the demise of one insignificant pump-station. I've even done a scenario for Baglan Bay Oil Refinery.'

'And what has it cost you?'

'Me? I've lived long enough to know when to turn off the lights and go home. I went round an old graveyard the other day, and you know what I noticed?'

'You're going to tell me anyway.' Charles was getting tired.

John Maples sipped his whisky and savoured the moment. 'I noticed that not one gravestone mentioned a person's qualifications, accomplishments or CV. As far as the tombstone's concerned, John Maples will only have lived because he was a son, a husband, a brother or a father.'

Charles looked away. The pressure of the last eighteen months had taken its toll. Charles Meddison was the company's bright young electronics expert with a growing department servicing its specialised computer needs. He'd left his beloved Yorkshire to live in a Houston suburb with his American wife Susan who was a doctor, and his twins Beth and Jenni. This life and this job were all that he'd ever wanted or hoped for.

Susan had grown up in Florida, in the beautiful seaside town of Fort Walton on the pan-handle and, following outstanding success at Florida State University, she had gone on to Princeton to study paediatrics.

That's where they'd met. He was doing a doctorate in electronic data interchange. Global had snapped him up from Cambridge, and generously sponsored him through the electronics doctorate programme. His expertise had great potential in the oil industry.

The last year had taken its toll. He had barely been home for months on end and, when he did get back to Houston he'd been so exhausted that all he wanted to do was sleep. Susan had a career, too, and she deeply resented his absence. His work was jeopardising her career as she'd had to spend more time at home with the twins than she'd wanted.

His visits home had been punctuated by stormy rows. He was too preoccupied or too mentally exhausted to take control of the situation, telling himself that after new year 2000 he'd go home for a long holiday and try to patch things up. On his last visit, however, things had been worse than ever and Susan had told him to move out to an hotel. As far as he could see he had blown it once and for all.

As the fine malt whisky cast its mellow spell over Charles Meddison he began to talk. He didn't really know John Maples, and what he did know he didn't particularly like. But still, he was affable enough and for the first time in months he realised how desperate he was to unload the burdens that he'd been carrying alone for so long.

'Do you ever wonder what it's for, John?'

Maples looked down into his glass and watched the whisky rippling under the movement of the jet. 'In my humble opinion, my Yorkshire friend, for most of the execs in Global it's simply about chasing the mighty buck.'

'Have I really just sunk eighteen months of my life, lost my wife and kids, messed up everything, just for bigger bucks?'

'Corporate loyalty maybe?' John Maples knew all about corporate loyalty. When corporations were falling apart and he was called in to rescue them he always majored on 'loyalty to the company'.

'That's rubbish, and you know it.' Charles poured himself another drink. 'The old ways are over. Heard of the Nobel prize-winner Ronald Coase?'

'The economist?' Maples kept abreast of the latest corporate gurus.

'He says that companies should only perform those functions which cannot be performed by the market.' Charles took a mouthful of whisky and savoured it.

'Moving everything out into cyberspace. Everything from buying and selling to designing products and hiring staff — even cleaning the office toilet?' Maples said.

'Yep. Corporate deconstruction theory. Don't do anything yourself that you can't get done cheaper somewhere else.' Charles had a note of irony in his voice.

Maples nodded. 'I've helped some companies to do it. Cannibalise your markets, treat your assets as liabilities, ensure continuity for the customer not for yourself.'

Charles smiled. 'Creative self-destruction.'

'Which means?'

Charles poured himself a third glass of whisky. 'Which means that Global Oil Networks couldn't really

101

give a damn about my marriage or my kids. In fact, they couldn't really give a damn about me. I reckon that as soon as this little panic's over they're going to deconstruct my department and put it out to tender.'

John Maples smiled knowingly and the conversation ended. Charles stared out of the window at the distant stars and the constant beam of the moon. He was filled with anomie, a sense of loss. Loss of his wife and loss of his kids. Since new year twelve months ago he had been presented with clear choices, and he'd chosen Global Oil Networks over Susan, Beth and Jenni. It was a choice which he bitterly regretted. For the remainder of the flight John Maples and Charles Meddison sat in silence, alone with their thoughts.

In less than twenty minutes the Lear was making its descent over the Worm and over Josh Lake's crackling bonfire hundreds of feet below. In that short space of time Charles Meddison and John Maples had consumed a lot more of the bottle of Glenfiddich, and had silently rehearsed their worst fears and nightmares for a new millennium.

The flashing beacon of Swansea airport was clearly visible from the window as they circled overhead, and the white lights which signalled the landing strip stretched out along the peninsula. The Lear cruised down and touched the runway with its backthrust roaring as it brought the jet to a deafening halt.

* * *

The Worm

Josh stoked the fire with a stick and a flurry of ash rose upwards. He was the leader, and it was his role to tend the fire. In this simple action he was connected to other bonfire builders. Other leaders.

As the flames licked heavenwards, Josh wondered whether the Brythons had even used this awesome place as their site for human sacrifice. They were a people who believed in reciprocity. To save a life, another must be given. Their world was peopled with the supernatural. They lived in a constant sense of the spiritual as well as the physical. It was a world of wonder and fear. Their worship was an ongoing ritual aimed at appeasing the powers made manifest in storms, thunder and lightning. Fire was the most revered aspect of their festivals, and Josh wondered how many bonfires they had lit on Worms Head to placate the gods after the harsh storms of winter.

He understood the primitive logic which motivated their human sacrifice, but he could never have participated in it himself. Somewhere, deep within him, the culture of 'fair play' which he had absorbed at public school resisted anything which smacked of cruelty.

'Can you hear anything, guys?' asked Josh.

There was silence.

'Can you hear horses' hooves and the clatter of wheels?'

'The what?' asked Jez, propping his head on his hand, and staring across at Josh in the flickering firelight.

'The ghost of Mr Mansel of Henllys, who's reputed to ride the Rhosili sands each night at midnight.' Josh was itching to tell them another story.

'No . . . but I think you might have heard the sea, lapping over the pathway to the Worm,' Jez said sarcastically.

Josh sprang to his feet and peered through the darkness. The sea was indeed rippling over the black rim of rock between the Worm and the headland. He turned back to Jez. 'What time is it? I looked up the tide table.

We should be fine till twelve thirty . . . .' But no one had a watch.

* * *

Anita Atwell blew out her candle and placed the blue pot gently back on the coffee table beside the veranda window. She looked out to sea towards the Worm, and saw the flickering flames of the bonfire still clearly visible. It wouldn't be long now. Soon the members of the community would be struggling back across the thin rim of rock towards Rhosili. She had better put the kettle on. They had promised to pop in for a cup of tea and to wish her happy new year on their return.

It was an unlikely relationship which Anita Atwell shared with the New Agers, yet it was a very special one. Anita wheeled her way into the kitchenette, with its low surfaces which she could use from wheelchair height. She liked the cottage, which had been left her by a favourite aunt, though without the help of Social Services she could never have lived in it. They had helped her to construct ramps and hand-rails, and a lovely new kitchen. It was now perfectly serviceable though still quite basic.

She had been in Rhosili for just over a year when Josh had first called at her door. His tightly cropped hair and long sideburns made him stand out in the small village of Rhosili and he hadn't found much of a welcome. They'd seen too many surfers and had too many bad experiences of kids sleeping rough in the area to want to help. No one had seemed of a mind to provide him with a field for the new community.

Just as he was waiting for the bus back to Swansea, however, Josh had noticed the orchard. It was an overgrown stretch of ground behind Anita's white-washed cottage, and on the gate was a newly painted sign on which was written 'Journey's End'.

Josh had knocked at the door several times, and was just about to leave when he heard the rattle of the wheelchair, and finally the door had squeaked open. Anita had smiled at him warmly, and he had stepped in to sit by the wood fire, drink tea and eat her Welsh cakes.

Anita had welcomed Josh as she would have welcomed anyone. Like Maidoc before her, Anita Atwell followed the hermit's rule of hospitality. Anyone was welcome, and she always gave of her best if they were willing to share a little of her simple life. In truth, however, Anita Atwell was also lonely. Any visitor, no matter who they were or what they looked like, would have been welcome that day and been offered fresh brewed tea and home-made Welsh cakes. When Josh and Anita met that September afternoon, two desperate people found one another.

It's strange how sometimes two people from different generations connect and find an instant rapport. That's the way it was that damp autumnal afternoon, as Anita Atwell and Joshua Lake warmed themselves by the crackling fire. Within a matter of minutes they had shared their lives and exchanged their stories. He told of parents too preoccupied with their careers to spend much time with him, of increasing distance between them and of days he spent bunking off private school in pursuit of adventure, dope and girls. He'd told of his suspension from school during his first year of 'A' levels, and then, after two attempts at returning, his expulsion from what was one of the most sought-after schools in the county.

He'd taken a 'year out', but it had really been an excuse to drop out and to explore a lifestyle which his parents found abhorrent. He went off for a few days at first, camping in his small one-man tent with travellers he'd met at the Reading Festival. Then he'd been introduced to an ecological protest, and had camped beside the River Thames along with scores of others in a protest to prevent the felling of a line of beautiful old oak trees which had graced the river bank for over a century.

His visits home had grown irregular, and he began to serve his apprenticeship in a New Age community based in the New Forest. He travelled from protest to protest and made his stand against ecological destruction, becoming well known by several police forces in the process.

He'd learnt a lot from his travelling companions — about life, about sex, about peace and about the power of Mother Earth. But now, at the age of twenty-eight, with daughters aged nine and twenty months in tow, he knew the time was right to stop the incessant travelling. Marie had urged him to create a community with more permanence, and had promised to support him in the formation of it.

Josh had downed his fourth Welsh cake before getting round to the real purpose of his visit. 'The orchard field . . . the one they call "Journey's End"?' He took a deep breath, his dark eyes peered at her.

'Yes?' She had already half-guessed what might be coming.

'The locals say it belongs to you, and I was wondering if we could make a kind of camp there, not a big one, just for the winter? And maybe in exchange we could keep the grass down, do some gardening, shopping, odd jobs and that. And help you out whenever you need anything.'

Anita Atwell chuckled. Her mind was already racing around the possibilities. She was a woman who liked to take risks. She always had been that way. Otherwise, why would a shy young girl from South Wales have gone to teach in Brixton?

Anita Atwell was always up for a challenge and loved to live on the edge. She knew full well that some of the village folk would object, but it was her land, and if it was only for a few months she would surely cope. And besides, she was lonely. Yes, they could make a start at forming a community at 'Journey's End' straight away.

* * *

Anita Atwell placed the cups and saucers on a tray, stripped the polythene off the plates of sandwiches and cakes she'd prepared earlier, and took the cans of beer from the fridge. She suspected that Josh Lake preferred beer to tea, and tonight, millennium night, was perhaps the right time to relax her rules about alcohol. She pressed the switch on the kettle and wheeled her way back to the veranda window.

She felt restless. If she had been well enough she would have put on her coat and strolled to the edge of the cliff and looked out to the Worm to see if they were all right. But things like that were beyond her now. She often felt deeply frustrated. There were places she wanted to go, people she wanted to meet, a life she wanted to live. But she was confined by the wheelchair and exhausted by the everyday jobs which once she'd done without thinking but which now demanded such supreme effort.

She peered out of the window. The fire was burning brighter now. That seemed odd, perhaps they were using up the rest of the wood before they left.

* * *

Some three miles away, out on the Worm, Josh and his friends were sitting in a circle having a meeting. Somewhere above there was the distant buzz of a plane, its wing and tail-lights clearly visible as it circled overhead.

The community always had a meeting when there was tension among them. Josh had learnt that lesson from communities of which he'd been a member. 'Talk don't fight' was the motto by which they lived. Community conferences were often deconstructionist, painful and even damaging to individuals, but voices were rarely raised. Talk was always seen as the best way forward.

Jez had lit another cigarette. 'I'm not friggin' sitting on the edge of this cliff for another four hours. You've gotta be joking. Besides, I need a joint.'

Josh sighed. 'As leader I'm telling you that we're staying put. All of us. There are rip tides around the ledge and it's very dark down there. We've got the fire. We stay put. Agreed?'

Suse looked at Jez pleadingly and the look was returned. 'If anyone wants to come with me, come now,' Jez said arrogantly. But no one stirred. Suse leant back and Scott placed his arm tenderly around her and squeezed her towards him.

Jez pushed his half-smoked cigarette into the grass and stubbed it out. Slowly he got up and strolled away down Devil's Bridge and out of sight. A few minutes later he had passed the tall reeds and reached the perilous ledge that was now almost submerged. He began the hazardous journey back to shore as the sea covered his big leather army boots.

The community sat in a circle looking at Josh. 'No one move. It's his action. His responsibility. His problem.'

Josh had learnt that in the peculiar style of leadership which New Agers exercise you never chased after anyone. People came and people went. True leaders never pulled rank over others, and never ran after those who left. Their focus always stayed on the ones who remained.

* * *

Charles reached forward and plucked the paper bag from the magazine rack in front of him. It simply read 'Global Oil Networks: Motion Discomfort'. Charles Meddison's discomfort was very real — and it was caused by hunger, adrenalin and Scots whisky mixed with the potent poison of regret. Deep regret. He felt as if he was going to die.

The shift manager from Baglan Bay was sitting in his car by the old run-down terminal building. As he saw Charles and John descend down the stairway from the plane's exit hatch he flashed his headlights. They both turned and strode towards him.

'Am I glad to see you guys!' smiled the shift manager. Charles slid unsteadily into the back seat. The manager reached out and warmly shook John Maples by the hand.

'Are you the techie?'

John Maples smiled. 'No. That's Charles. But let him sleep for a while, he's very tired.'

They drove off quickly. Charles Meddison's head was swimming. He was trying to arrange a plethora of different thoughts and images into some kind of order in his head.

As they sped off into the night the manager began to lay out the details of the crisis. 'Up to last year each of the individual plants had its own control room. They've been retained but equipped with data collection equipment. An interface system in each control room now connects by underground cable to the central control room.'

Charles Meddison grunted, his mind not really registering the importance of the information. The manager continued.

'The data highway from each of the data collection points is duplicated to minimise the risk of accidental damage or failure. So each of the cabling systems leaves each unit and travels to the control room by completely different routes. The control room even has its own stand-by generating set.'

Charles grunted again. Mental images of data highways, control rooms and generators were swirling before him.

'The computer system is Honeywell. We've got terminals to read the status in each refining unit, and a supervisory panel to take readings from the entire system. Two mainframes control different aspects, but the larger computer oversees and co-ordinates them. The individual control rooms are unmanned, but central control can direct operatives to any point in the system. We also have full VDU facilities in the technical office, and we can access the entire system from there, too.'

The manager was in a big hurry. He was driving at over sixty miles an hour over deserted country roads that wound their way along the coastline of the Gower and led towards the old fishing port of Mumbles and Swansea beyond. As they swung round a particularly acute left-hand bend the headlights picked out the distant shape of a man. He was standing in the middle of the road and waving his arms. The car skidded to a halt only feet away from the shadowy figure.

Charles Meddison looked out through his alcoholic haze and saw what looked like a ghost. It was Jez, still dripping wet from his struggle against the rip tides around Worms Head. His arm was gashed and bleeding from the rocks he'd clambered up to reach the road above.

Jez approached the window and the shift manager wound it down for just an inch.

'Help. I need help. I was stranded out there on Worm Island, and I've just got back. I've cut my arm real bad.'

Instinctively Charles Meddison pushed open the rear door. 'Get in, we're in a hurry, we'll get it sorted.'

The manager turned round, his eyes piercing, even in the darkness. 'What the hell are you doing?'

'Simple public relations, isn't that right, John?'

'Yep, that's right Charles.' John Maples could already see the headline. 'Oil executives save drowning man in refinery crisis.' John smiled. Perhaps Charles Meddison wasn't quite as drunk as he'd imagined.

* * *

The Worm

Josh and his friends were seated on the edge of the Worm, watching the dying embers of their millennium bonfire. The roaring flames which had lit up the night sky an hour previously had gone, and their supply of wood was all but exhausted.

Marie slowly sprinkled the last bag of sawdust onto the fire and it flickered into life for one last brief time. Josh cuddled Pol in his arms. She was fast asleep, and Jem was huddled close to him. And so they sat, looking at the dying embers, and dreading the long night before them.

'Josh,' Marie whispered, 'don't you think we should find some shelter? I mean, if we could get out of the breeze and cuddle together, wouldn't it be better for the kids?'

Scott stood up. 'And where the hell would we find shelter around here, we're on the edge of the world!'

111

Josh cuddled Pol tight. 'Any caves nearby?'

Marie smiled. This was her territory. The place where she'd grown up, and she knew the ridges and crevasses of the Worm better than anyone.

'No problem, I know a cave which nobody else knows.'

The last flickering flames of the fire disappeared and only embers remained. Josh held Pol tight in his arms. The child was sound asleep. He slowly stood, little Jem stood too, and she hugged him around the waist.

'OK. I'll buy that. We're going to get very cold if we stay here.'

So the bedraggled little procession set out. Marie was at the front carrying a torch which was flickering because its battery was nearly dead. Then came Josh carrying Pol, with Scott and Suse walking hand in hand with Jem.

It wasn't an easy path but Marie knew it well, and she led them from Outer Head across the ridge of Devil's Bridge and on towards Middle Worm.

Even as they began to edge across Devil's Bridge a strange eerie sound started to echo round the rocks. 'What the hell's that?' Scott sounded jumpy.

'It's only the blow hole,' Marie called over her shoulder. 'The tide must have turned, and as the water enters the crevasse it pushes air up the funnel in the rocks. Hiss . . . boom . . . Hear it?'

Marie shone the flickering torch down a grassy slope from the main path. 'Here's the cave.'

'How d'you know about it?' Josh felt slightly disappointed that it wasn't his idea.

'We used to come here when I was a kid, sit on this balcony, and look at the seals below.'

They gently edged their way down the grassy bank. It was very slippery and the towering cliffs by the reed grass dropped away suddenly to the sea below. Marie triumphantly shone her torch into the deep cave beside the grassy ledge. 'Home sweet home.'

The six of them huddled together in the cave, wrapping their coats around each other to ensure that the children were protected from the damp and cold. Somewhere deep in the cave they could hear the sound of running water. They assumed it was the sound of a stream.

Marie shone the torch around the dark rocky walls, as if for reassurance.

'Reckon the cave dwellers lived here?' Scott asked.

'Who knows?' Josh liked to be an authority on history. 'But the Sweyn's burial houses on Rhosili Down date from 4,000 BC.'

'And the Penmaen Burrows in the dunes are about that old, too.' Marie wasn't going to be outdone.

Marie continued to shine the torch around the walls, as if to uncover some ancient cave drawing as yet undiscovered. But there was nothing but rock.

'Sorry guys, but I've just got to pee,' said Suse, standing up so that a cold draft enveloped the circle.

Marie shone the torch deeper into the cave. 'The ladies loo is straight ahead.' Suse grabbed the torch.

'I'm not going in there without the torch.' She slowly moved forward, crouching under the low rocky ceiling. Suddenly the torch brightened, drawing strength from some remaining cell.

As she pointed the torch towards the inner wall of the cave it revealed the deeply carved shape of a Celtic cross, and beneath it a table hewn out from the dense rock face.

'What the heck?' Suse stopped in her tracks, the torchlight trained on the cross.

Scott smiled. 'Don't know about cave men, but I reckon the Church of England got here first.'

St Thomas's Hospital. London

Paperwork is important at St Thomas's Hospital. No paperwork means no information. And a lack of information about a patient slows things down and frustrates everyone involved.

There was no paperwork on Dave Rushden. No one had been able to discover his name, address, age, next of kin, religion, or doctor's address.

The girl on reception had filled in the computer registration as 'Details unknown. Male. Head injury. Arrived by ambulance from Downing Street, SW1.' Even as she had entered the data she smiled. Perhaps he was someone important, but then, looking at his long unkempt hair, his denim shirt and jeans, and faded jacket, it was rather unlikely. His clothes had certainly seen better days.

Every member of staff who came into contact with him had asked his name, but all to no avail. It somehow seemed inappropriate to address someone so simply dressed as 'sir'.

Dave Rushden endured a whole range of medical tests to identify exactly what was wrong with him. It had begun in A and E with the Glasgow coma test in which the houseman had shone a torch into his eyes to establish whether the pupils were dilated, and pin-pricks had been administered to his feet to test his reflexes.

By 2 am his condition had been considered serious enough to warrant a CT scan. It was a matter of some urgency to determine whether there was any swelling in the brain and to search for any sign of a blood clot. The scanner was at the far end of the hospital, a full ten minutes ride by trolley from Accident and Emergency. PC

Breeson, Dave Rushden's police escort, accompanied him to the scanner, aware that he might do a runner. If his charge escaped there would be hell to pay.

The CT scanner produced pictures of Dave Rushden's brain. Coloured pictures. Pictures which to a layman appeared to be no more than bright patterns within a skull-shaped boundary, but which to a trained eye revealed much more.

* * *

The Venerable James Roberts had talked to Dave about the brain. They'd been arguing about it. They were walking along Rhosili beach, and the surf was up. James had nearly finished his thesis, but he still felt he had much to learn from Dave's peculiar New Age perspective on things.

'James. You've got to learn how to place your thinking mind on hold so that you can perceive the subtle energies.' Dave was urgent. Focused.

'That's rubbish, and you know it.' James had come across an aspect of New Age theory which he considered nonsense.

'We must still the wordy chatter of our left hemisphere so that we can become aware of the messages from the silent, mystical half. That's how we get in touch with the deepest reality.'

James felt irritated. 'Look, a lot of what you say makes sense, but this is where I draw the line. If New Age empowerment can only come by shutting down my rational, critical filter, my mind, then I just can't buy it.'

'James, you've got to short-circuit the rational mind and tune in your mind at large.'

'Rubbish. The greatest endowment of the human mind is its ability to discriminate between what is true and what is false. To verify what is real and to throw out what is delusion.'

'But what's that got to do with genuine spirituality?' Dave was puzzled.

'Everything, Dave. Everything. Humans are rational beings, and our correspondence with God is in that rationality. If God created the human mind and gave us the ability to reason . . . it's logical to assume that we can understand his revelation to us intellectually.' James was restraining himself, he felt he was preaching.

'So what does that have to do with me?' Dave was genuinely interested.

'It means that God wants you to use your mind. Not only to ask if Christian spirituality feels good, but if it's true.'

'But surely we need to be silent within as well.' Dave's voice was full of compassion, but his words challenged James at the deepest level.

James Roberts' life in the church had been full of words. Words of theology, words of liturgy, words of hymnody. His had been a religion of words, but in reality he hungered for a religion of silence. A religion in which the awesome Word of God could break through and speak to him.

James and Dave paused and watched the white surf racing up the beach towards them. They were standing and looking out to sea. Only the gulls interrupted the loud silence. Perhaps he and Dave were both right after all. Perhaps logic and linear thinking can only take you so far.

Perhaps in the end, at the end, you must face the silence in which God speaks. The Word breaking into human experience. There, on the smooth sandy beach at Rhosili, James and Dave shared that silence together.

Some thirty minutes later Dave Rushden was back in the A and E cubicle. PC Breeson took the small plastic bag which contained all of his personal effects and trawled through them again. If nothing else, he hoped that the patient might object. Any reaction seemed better than this silence. Rushden remained immobile . . . staring up at the wall-clock in front of him.

The plastic bag didn't reveal much about Dave's identity. It contained twenty-five pounds sterling, a small silver Celtic cross, a return coach ticket to Swansea for 2.30 pm on 1 January 2000, a pocket-sized A to Z of London, and a small visiting card which read 'Sisters of the Seashore, Anita Atwell, Journey's End, Worm's Head Path, Rhosili, The Gower, Swansea'.

PC Breeson shook the London A to Z, and out dropped a photograph of a couple standing outside an old army tent. They looked deliriously happy.

'Who's this then. Wife, mistress, lover . . . your ex? Who?'

Dave looked at the picture. He recognised himself but had no recollection of the woman. She was beautiful, happy, young. It was Eva, the great love of his life. The woman who had dominated his thinking, who had affected him more than any other and with whom he'd shared the greatest moments of his life. But now he simply did not recognise her.

Perhaps, at last, this loss of memory would be the resolution of his heartbreak. The ending of the pain which had accompanied him like some ceaseless noise for the last three months. Perhaps, at last, he could erase the last look of those large brown eyes. The look that cracked his heart. Perhaps he was ready to move on to the rest of his life.

When you lived the transient kind of life that David Rushden lived, you travelled light. He had travelled that way ever since leaving his last foster home and setting off for university. He had travelled light because there was nothing and nobody from his childhood which he had wished to carry with him.

His father had died when he was eight and soon afterwards his mother had moved in with a man whom she loved but came to fear. Life had become a nightmare, and Dave's disruptive behaviour at school had finally brought him to the attention of Social Services.

They'd never been able to prove his step-father's violence, but the social work team were alert enough to recognise that Dave's home life was disturbed, and that the family was seriously dysfunctional. He had been moved 'into care', and as the years went by he saw his mother less and less. He grew up young, and learnt that if he didn't make his own way in the world that no one would do it for him.

His commitment to the Mother Earth group was total, and he travelled extensively among the various New Age communities in the south of England recruiting new support and planning campaigns. They were, in a sense, his family. They were the people to whom he belonged and from whom he gained his sense of worth and his identity as a person.

Whatever few possessions he had were stored in his old army tent back at 'Journey's End' in the Gower. He'd seen the power of possessions. The squabbles in communities over who owned what. The fevered race to acquire more and more after his peers left university. The dulling effect which possessions had on the middle class. He felt that those who owned the most only cared the least. Many human beings were trapped by their need to possess things and were, in effect, possessed by what they owned.

He believed that possessions were a corrupting influence. They built walls between people. They became a source of security, an end in themselves. Parents plied their young with possessions but neglected to give them the things for which they craved. Security, love and sensitivity.

Since late September Dave had always come back to Rhosili and to his friends in the community on the Gower. If people asked where he lived he always spoke of Anita Atwell's orchard as home. He liked Josh, but there had been growing tension between them. They both worked out their New Age philosophy in different ways. He was grateful that, at least, Josh allowed him to come and go, but felt that the arrangement would soon come to an end. Dave loved the Gower, too, and in some strange way he saw it as the kind of landscape which would one day dominate the British Isles again.

PC Breeson turned back to the trolley. 'So, who's this Anita Atwell? And who are these Sisters of the Seashore?'

Dave Rushden looked blankly at the wall-clock.

'Come on. You must remember something. An address, a phone number, a wife?'

Dave Rushden's eyes moved slowly to focus on the young fresh-faced face peering down at him.

'Pig.' Dave sneered.

Instinctively the officer unclipped the handcuffs that were secured to his belt and in one brisk smooth movement snapped them shut. Dave Rushden's left wrist was securely locked to the metal trolley on which he lay. The officer smiled, turned, and strolled out of the cubicle. The black plastic doors flapped shut behind him.

Whatever else he had forgotten, Dave Rushden had not forgotten his hatred of authority. It was so deeply ingrained within him that, even though he didn't remember his own name, he knew he hated those in power whoever they were.

This hatred had been reinforced in his early days as a political activist at university. He'd considered himself a law-abiding citizen until, during one demo, he'd been arrested and hauled off to the cells by two enthusiastic young officers. One had stood behind him, gripping his arms, while the other had punched him in the stomach.

From then on the police were the enemy. Pigs. The army of the state, being used to control the population without even knowing it. They were uniforms. Men hiding behind batons, shields and armour-plated minibuses. He'd never known a policeman, and he never wanted to.

Note

1. 'I see His blood upon the rose' was written in the early part of this century by Joseph Mary Plunkett. (Plunkett, Joseph Mary, 1934, in *Prose and Poetry of England*, H. Ward McGraw, ed. [The Singer Company: Chicago].)

CHAPTER 4
The Dark Hours

The Vicarage. Wandsworth, London

It was 3.20 am, and James Roberts was wide awake. He was not usually an insomniac. His job was so demanding and so time-consuming that he could fill every waking hour with endless activity. There was never normally enough sleep.

Helen was in bed and fast asleep, but James was still high on adrenaline and anxiety. He wandered into his book-lined study, took the sermon notes out of his prayerbook, leafed through them, and placed them carefully in the back of a file marked 'Sermons. Advent Season 1999'. He had a sense that what had happened at Westminster Abbey had somehow been a watershed. It was as if everything before it had just been a preparation for that occasion, that sermon, that millennium moment.

He turned and looked along the shelves and pulled out a dusty book. He sat down at his desk, turned on the desk lamp and began to read *The Lives of the Celtic Saints*.

Maidoc inherited the practice of living a solitary life in a remote place from the mystics of the Egyptian desert. The hermit's withdrawal was not a flight or escape from the difficulties of life. Maidoc withdrew from the normal routine of life in order to confront its suffering. His prayers were to help others. His main concern was with the lot of those who were making journeys, both in terms of travel, and in terms of the spiritual pilgrimage of life. In recent years there has been a resurgence of the hermit disciplines, and particularly in parts of Wales, North-Western Scotland and the Shetland Islands.

James Roberts gently placed the open book on his desk and leant back in his swivel chair, his hands in his pockets. He looked out over the lights of London spread before him. James loved London, the buzz of it, the excitement of it, the sense of being at the centre of the action. But how could he make his new sense of God work in such an urban setting? He picked up the book again.

Increasingly, we are being liberated from the oppressive mores and constricting institutional organisations of our forefathers. We are beginning to find ourselves adrift in a world where science, which once promised better standards of life, is now unable to control its own power and has become a force for destruction. When so many are looking East to find an answer, we must look back to the ancient traditions of our own lands, to find a tradition that might show us how we can find peace in this world and a new sense of the transcendent. We need to learn from ancient Celtic leaders like Maidoc.

James knew that Maidoc had found on Worm's Head a perfect place of isolation and inaccessibility. During the day he meditated on the holy patriarchs, the prophets, the apostles and the martyrs, and during the night he looked towards his eternal destiny with patience and cheerful hope. Perhaps, James Roberts mused, he might become a kind of new millennium Maidoc for Wandsworth. Perhaps he could carve out a style of Christian ministry based in prayer, a life of inner quiet, even in the noise and bustle of London. He desperately wanted Christ to be at the centre of his ministry. He picked up the book again.

Maidoc considered despair to be among the deadliest of sins, so disciplined himself to look on life with hope and joy. He saw silence as a strength, and he lived by a rule in which he could not speak before he was asked a question. Prayer and contemplation were his daily work, and he invested everything in doing them well. The emptiness of his cave was a symbol of the inner silence which he invited Christ to fill.

James looked around him at the thick pile carpet, the walls lined with books, the computer and fax on the desk before him, and the city bustle beyond. He wondered if he could really discover such a simple stillness in this urban environment. He recognised that the discovery of such a silence was, perhaps, his greatest contribution to the life of the Church and the life of the world. It was more important than being a good middle manager for the religious institution. What good was a priest unable to pause for a moment, let alone a lifetime. He read on.

Maidoc's chief enemy was anger, which he considered the cause of all distraction. He believed that a man of prayer who gives way to anger is like a man who wishes to see clearly but who scratches at his eyes. He was tormented by hordes of demons. He had withdrawn from the activity of the world in order to confront its suffering. He prayed that he might help others, especially those who were spiritually on their way towards God. Many made long journeys to seek his help. He lived by the rule that he who knows himself knows God.

James Roberts gently placed the book down. Did he know himself? Did he really understand who he was in God? Or did he only know the religious persona, the role he could portray so convincingly to everyone who came his way? Finally, the mix of adrenalin and caffeine having dissipated, James Roberts gave way to sleep. He was slumped in his chair, his head bowed down. And he dreamt of Maidoc. The Celtic priest. His hero.

Maidoc, the hermit, was huddled in a corner of his cave and his eyes blazed like fire. Maidoc was looking at him. Staring at him. James felt that the hermit could see right through him. James had made the perilous journey across the rocky ridge of his imagination to dream of Maidoc.

Maidoc rose from his straw bedding in the corner of the hermit cave. He marked the day, as he did each morning, with a simple sign on the wall. He was now in his fourth year of the desert discipline.

He had chosen this cave because it faced west and looked towards the horizon where the sun would set each day, and because its inner wall faced east. Maidoc prostrated himself on the dusty ground before the little altar and the carved stone cross facing east. And as he prayed he shook. He shook with such violence that he tried to grasp the ground as it moved beneath him.

They had come for him again, the demons of the night. He felt himself attacked by them, a whole army of cursed devils banded together against him. Only with the most resolute courage could he stand his ground. The creatures had great heads, long necks, faces adorned with filthy matted beards, distorted expressions, fierce eyes, foul mouths, and their teeth were like those of horses.

Maidoc was sometimes sick with deprivation, ill with fever, hungry, thirsty, and frustrated by solitude. But all his earthly sufferings were as nothing compared to the horrors of the supernatural. They had come across Devil's Bridge, and they had come for him.

'In the name of Jesus Christ, the Saviour and Redeemer of the world. Be gone. Be gone back across

Devil's Bridge. Be gone. By the blood of the Saviour. By the power of God's Spirit. By the forces of the angelic host. Be gone. Be gone.'

Suddenly Maidoc was still. He looked exhausted, his face dripping with sweat, and his steaming breath rising in the chill morning air. Tears streamed down into his matted beard. Slowly he turned to face James Roberts, and he looked deep into his eyes.

The dream was over. Maidoc was gone. James Roberts awoke. Only the street lights remained. James leant back in his chair and whispered, 'Lord Jesus, I would be wholly yours. Demons of the night. Be gone. Be gone. Be gone.' It was 4.10 am.

* * *

The cottage. Rhosili

By 3.30 am Anita Atwell was consumed with worry. She wheeled herself over to the lounge table, picked up the phone, dialled 999 and asked for the coastguard.

Within seconds she was connected to an operator in a coastguard unit over seventy miles away. She explained the situation. 'It's the children, that's why I'm so worried. Only nine years and twenty months. If they're stranded by the tide they could catch their death. It's such a cold night.'

'Look, we're very stretched here tonight,' came the man's warm reply, 'and it's only an hour till they can cross on the ridge. Sit tight and call us again in an hour if there's no news. OK?'

Anita Atwell said, 'OK,' but she didn't feel OK. She felt restless and uneasy. She had resisted the impulse for long enough. The time had come to wake her other colleagues and call on them to pray. She phoned them one by one and explained the situation. Two of them were already up and saying the morning liturgy.

Each Sister agreed to pray for Josh and the community at 4 am. The Sisters of the Seashore were used to urgent cries for help such as this. It was part of their calling to respond by day or by night. It was an integral part of their life.

The Sisters each lived alone and in secluded places. They all followed the simple hermit lifestyle of the Desert Fathers. They obeyed the discipline of the desert with its austere lifestyle and emphasis on prayer. It was a discipline which first arrived in South Wales in the fifth century and which became such an enriching force in the life of the Celtic church.

The Sisters of the Seashore hadn't accepted Anita without reservations. There were always those who wanted to share their hermit vocation because they were running away from heartbreak or from life's bitter disappointments. But slowly Mother Superior had discerned in Anita the quality which the Sisters looked for among those who desired to join them. A hunger for God and a desire for his presence in every waking hour.

Slowly Anita discovered that a life of intercession is not an easy option. Back in Brixton she had given herself to the care of thirty-two children from nine ethnic backgrounds in a school starved of funds . . . and that had been difficult. But this life of intercession was just as hard, in some ways harder.

The Sisters of the Seashore was founded by an ex-Franciscan nun called Sister Alexandra in 1935. It consisted of a rather odd mix of women, some of whom had taken holy orders and some who had not. All of them, however, had pledged to live alone, to pray and to seek after God. Each of them adopted the specific disciplines of a different Celtic saint. Anita had chosen Maidoc,

whose name was enshrined in the Gower village of
Llanmadoc, and who was trained under the Irish monk
Aidan. He had adopted the Irish name Maidoc because
it was a nickname for Aidan. He had originated from
Llangennith, and was sent by the Christian community
there to train in the monasteries of Ferns, Drumlane and
Rossinver, later returning to Wales to pray for his home-
land.

Anita modelled her spirituality on Maidoc's discipline of contemplation which was focused on the heart
rather than the mind. This, ultimately, was Maidoc's
greatest contribution to Celtic spirituality.

It was 4.00 am and Anita was sitting back beside
the veranda window and looking out at the night sky. She
was praying. Praying for the safety of the children.
Praying for Jez. Praying for Dave Rushden. Praying for
Josh Lake. Praying for them all as she did at about that
time every morning.

Anita Atwell would never have discovered this ministry of prayer if it had not been for her multiple sclerosis.
In her former life as a junior school teacher she had filled
each day with practical deeds and caring service in the
hurting inner-city community. She'd had little time for
prayer then.

She still ached for that old life. She missed it with a
longing which draped itself around her during every waking hour. But that chapter of her life was over and prayer
was the doorway to the next. She looked at the mis-
shapen candle on the bright blue pot coated in wax. Her
life sometimes felt like that candle. Melted, broken, mis-
shapen. But daily she prayed that somehow God would
mould a new shape for her life and enable her to burn
solely for him.

She had left the main stage and was now called to
stand invisibly in the wings. She was called to live like an

angel, unknown and unappreciated, and to pour out her life in prayer for anyone in need. And the struggles she faced in this new life were mainly within herself.

The greatest struggle wasn't the illness, nor even the loneliness. It was her struggle with the demons of the night. Mother Superior had taught her about these dark forces and Anita had read and reread the Bible passages describing how best to fight them. But she had never imagined it would be like this. Day upon endless day they came across Devil's Bridge to seek her out and to test her faith and calling.

Even as she prayed on millennium night they came. They came as regret. Regret over the man she'd loved but never married. Regret about what could have been. The life she could have lived. The children she might have borne.

And they came as failure. Scenes from the classroom. Innocent faces. Hurting eyes. Opportunities missed. Good deeds left undone. A sense of having lived only half a life when once she had the strength to do much more.

And then as fear. Revealing the future as some dark horror of what might be. The doctor had put it bluntly, 'Multiple sclerosis can be a wasting disease with seasons of remission.' But what did wasting mean? A twisted body in a geriatric ward, gasping for breath and wishing to die. Vivid images of future suffering.

They came in her need to be loved. The need to be held tight and to feel the warm touch of another. The hunger for tender words. Affirmation. Appreciation for who she was and what she might become.

Anita was no stranger to tears, but that night, millennium night, she was so exhausted by these fightings without and within that she was too tired to cry. Yet her whole body shook with grief. She struggled with her dark valley of sorrows and prayed that Christ would bring her through.

The demons which had haunted Maidoc visited Anita on millennium night. And, just as the hermit had done on Worm's Head fifteen hundred years before, she called out in the terrors of the night. 'In the name of Jesus Christ. Be gone. Be gone. Be gone.' It was 4.10 am.

* * *

The Worm

Suse returned and the circle of cold, tired bodies closed again to include her. 'It's creepy in here,' she said, shivering.

'Don't be stupid,' said Josh. 'It's great. Connection with the past. These walls speak.'

Josh had a habit of being poetic when people needed reassurance. Pol was still safely tucked in his arms, but as Suse re-entered the circle Pol's bright eyes opened wide and she let out a fearful and piercing scream which echoed deep into the cave beyond. Worst of all, the scream did not end. Its resonating echo continued unabated. Sometimes it had a high pitch and sometimes low, but always ear-piercing and constant. Its echo ringing and reverberating around the walls.

Jem began to shake, perhaps affected by the desperate cry of her tiny sister, or perhaps exhausted by a day too long for any nine-year-old to cope with. The shaking was gentle at first but gradually it grew more violent until it rocked the others in the circle and became an uncontrollable spasm.

Josh spoke firmly but loudly, 'Girls, girls, quiet, quiet. It's all OK, I'm here.' Whether the fear within Pol was triggered by the darkness or by some other deep and indescribably infant fear they couldn't know.

Suse stood up again and the scant warmth of their closeness was broken. 'This is like a bad trip . . . this is like cold turkey . . . this is heavy . . . get me out of here . . . get me out of here.'

Scott stood and tried to comfort her in a warm embrace but she pushed him away. 'Get away from me, leave me alone. I should have gone with Jez. This place is unreal, it's not right, get us out of here. Josh, get us out of here.'

Marie pulled Jem towards her. She wanted to hold the child and to comfort her, but Jem's reaction was instantaneous and dramatic. She sprang back from Marie and lay on the ground in the foetal position, still shaking violently. Then she began to whimper.

Josh stood, still holding Pol, and walked to the entrance of the cave. The screaming continued, the like of which he had never heard in his life before. Josh stood with the young child in his arms and looked out to sea. It was still very dark.

Suse was growing hysterical. Over and over again she said, 'Bad trip . . . bad trip . . . cold turkey,' her breathing rapid and shallow. She was hyperventilating.

'Get them away from me,' she shrieked. 'Get those teeth away . . . get away . . . get away . . . .'

Josh looked back into the cave. Marie was kneeling beside Jem. Suse was walking back and forth. Scott was following her and speaking words of reassurance. This, indeed, was a bad trip.

At exactly 4.10 am Josh heard a cry far louder than Pol's which echoed towards him from deep within the inner cave. 'In the name of Jesus Christ, Saviour and Redeemer. Be gone. Be gone. Be gone.'

Instantly Pol was silent. Jem lay completely still, she was calm again and the whimpering had stopped. Suse stood safe in Scott's arms. Marie was smiling at him.

'Bad trip over?' asked Josh.

'Bad trip over.' Marie replied.

'Then I think it's time we made a move. The tide's going down.'

And so the little procession began again. They scrambled up the grassy bank, over the steep mound of Middle Worm, and down onto the rocky footpath that had just appeared above the level of the calm smooth sea. It was still very dark, and Marie shone the torch back and forth along the footpath so that everyone could safely place their feet in the damp narrow track.

As they edged their way along, with Josh holding Pol, and Suse gripping Jem's hand, Suse dare not voice what she was thinking. Had Jez been swept out to sea from this same path just a few hours before?

'What the hell's that?' shouted Scott pointing across the sea towards Swansea. The sky was lit up by streaks of bright orange light and streams of tiny bright sparks shooting up into the sky.

'Looks like a firework display,' sighed Josh, 'must be pretty good if we can see it from here!'

'What? At this time in the morning? I think not!' Marie was so gripped by the sight that she was pointing the torch into thin air towards Swansea.

'Some sort of distress flare?' Scott was always imaginative.

'Maybe they're all looking for us!' Josh mused.

'Somehow I doubt it,' smiled Marie. 'Could be the Port Talbot steelworks, but the flares never go up that high.'

'Or the Baglan Bay Refinery?' suggested Scott.

'I sincerely hope not!' said Josh. The procession edged slowly forward. The rocks were still very slippery. Twenty minutes later they had arrived at their little encampment. It was very basic, but they looked on it as

131

home. The grass in the orchard was overgrown and full of weeds. It was wet with dew as it was most mornings. Marie's torch picked out their paltry dwellings in among the apple trees.

In one corner of the orchard was Dave Rushden's old army tent. Its brown and green camouflage made it blend into the orchard setting so that it was barely visible. Dave had bought it from an army surplus shop in Swansea, and he liked the idea that something made for war was now being used by a community dedicated to peace.

Josh, Marie and the kids lived in a tepee near Anita's cottage. He'd had it made by one of the girls in the New Forest community when he'd first moved in with Meena. Inside it seemed much more roomy than it appeared from the outside. Beside it was an old igloo tent, where they kept food, provisions and firewood.

Suse and Scott had the most basic accommodation. It was a strange structure made out of wood and tarpaulin which was leaning against three trees in the orchard. It was waterproof, and inside the bedroom was lined with layers of old tent canvas. The interior was decorated with ornately patterned batik which Scott had bought when travelling through Malaysia.

Josh was still carrying Pol, whose weight had now become a heavy burden. He was determined to hold her until she could be laid in her bed. He walked through the long wet grass to Jez's hut. It was a rough structure made of old sheets of plywood nailed together. Jez had always liked working with wood, and this was his home.

Josh pushed the door open with his foot and peered inside. Jez's sleeping bag was empty. He hoped against hope that Jez had made it. But now he felt for sure that Jez was dead.

Josh walked on past the big old bell tent, which had

seen better days. It had been patched and sewn together in a haphazard way. This was the space where Josh met the community to talk, to listen, to share, and to recite the great legends of the Celtic people.

As soon as Jem and Pol were laid down in their sleeping bags they were asleep, it had been a long and eventful day for them. Josh pulled his poncho around him and strolled down the beaten grass pathway to Anita's cottage. It was just after 5 am and all the cottage lights were on.

Josh knocked gently on the back door and pushed it open. It squeaked in its familiar reassuring way.

'Anita, it's me, Josh . . . we're back.'

'Come in, come in.' Anita called. 'Thank God you're safe. Thank God. Thank God.'

'Has Jez been back?'

'No . . .' Anita could detect the concern in his voice. 'Why?'

Josh stood by the door, looking awkward, and not meeting her eyes. 'He's gone. We got cut off by the tide, but he wouldn't wait. He just left.'

'We'd better call the coastguard . . . and the police.'

Josh didn't reply. The authorities just spelt trouble. 'Call them if you want.'

He slunk out of Anita Atwell's lounge, head bowed. It had not been a good night.

Josh crept back across the wet grass and pulled open the flap of the tepee. He kicked off his wet boots, pulled the poncho over his head and slipped into the double sleeping bag next to Marie.

'OK?' she whispered.

'No, I feel scared,' he whispered in reply.

She held him close, nursing his head against her shoulder and gently stroking his head. It was a rare moment in their relationship. Josh, the strong leader on whom everyone else depended, now needed someone to be strong for him.

'Don't be scared, I'm here for you,' she whispered.

Tears welled up within him and for the first time in many years they poured down his face in a great river of emotion. Marie held him, her fingers gently stroking his hair. He could hear the strong steady beat of her heart.

'Tell me, tell me, if you want to, and I will hear you. I am here for you my strong, gentle man.' Her Welsh whisper sounded like a poem.

'What is this life, and why is it so quickly gone?' he whispered. 'And what have I done with my life?'

Marie gently rocked him. 'So many lovers, so many places, so many sorrows,' she said as she gently kissed his forehead. 'Nothing solid, nothing to hold on to.'

'And tonight, in the cave, I had a bad trip, too,' he whispered.

'But you seemed so calm.'

'Only on the outside.' For Josh the voice in the cave had been a moment of ultimate reality.

'And is it time to stop running now, my gentle love?' She held him even tighter.

'Maybe . . . but I'm scared. I've never been more scared in my life.'

* * *

St Thomas's Hospital. London

The white screen flickered on and Dr Jane Jennings clipped three films from Dave's CT scan to it. She didn't like the dark shade above the patient's right temple. It always intrigued her that an injury to the back of the head generally results in a second injury to the front. The brain, a three-pound substance resembling thick por-

ridge, lies suspended in liquid. When it is jarred it moves
. . . and serious damage is done when it impacts the skull.
She flicked off the neon display. It was time to call in the
duty neurologist.

At about 3.50 Sergeant Stephens from Alpha 4
burst through the rubber doors to check on John
Breeson's progress with his prisoner. He was tense and
fed up. He looked down at Rushden.

'Look here, we've got all your mates. We know what
you were doing. Now, tell us . . . name and address . . .
and we'll get you out of here.'

Dave looked up and smiled.

'It's no good. He's blotto,' said PC Breeson.

'Name . . . savvi . . . name . . . you speak English?'

Dave pulled himself up and tugged at the cuffs
which held his left wrist to the trolley. He was beginning
to get agitated. The side of the trolley was shaking, and
he was struggling to get free.

'I think we'd better make sure you don't go anywhere, Mr Nobody.'

The sergeant unclipped his handcuffs, pulled Dave's
right arm down, and snapped them shut round his right
wrist. He was now spead-eagled across the trolley, tightly
secured by both wrists.

'Outside.' The sergeant beckoned to his junior; and
they both sauntered out of the cubicle. They were going
for a smoke in the police car.

As they left and the rubber doors clicked shut
behind them Dave started to wriggle and then to writhe.
Something was disturbing him and it didn't look pleasant.

Dave saw the tall dark figure of a man looming
towards him. The man was silhouetted and he looked like
a giant. In one hand he was carrying a belt, and with the
other he was lifting Dave by the wrist. Dave's feet were off
the ground.

Dave Rushden was a child again. Eight years old . . . and his drunk and violent step-father was angry. It was night. It was dark. He was very tired.

He felt the agony again as he was lifted from the bed by his wrist and hauled along. He was wriggling and writhing, trying to get free, but the other wrist was gripped, too. The man threw him over his knee, clamping down his back with one arm while raising the belt with the other.

'I told you that I'd take the belt to you. I said I'd do it and I meant it . . . stay still you little brat, stay still. You don't really belong here, you know that, don't you.'

The human mind is a strange and complex organism. To all intents and purposes Dave's memory of everything over the last eighteen years had been erased, but as is the case with retrograde amnesia, childhood memories remain crystal clear, perhaps more vivid than ever before. The dark silhouette was the frightening shape of authority in the shadowy form of his drunken step-father.

Dr Jennings heard the screams and came racing through the doors. She looked aghast at Dave writhing and rolling on the bed, tied by his wrists to the trolley and screaming like a child.

Dave Rushden was encountering the demons of his past. The dark forces which had moulded his childhood view of the world and which had shaped his destiny. They were horrifying and real, and they had returned again and again across the years to haunt him.

Within seconds four members of staff were helping to restrain the patient while Jane Jennings injected a sedative to calm him down. It was 4.10 am.

Jane Jennings was very, very angry. 'Who the hell gave permission for him to be trussed up like some turkey? God only knows what harm's been done.'

Meanwhile, outside, the two policemen moaned

about the prisoner, about the lousy night, about the pressures of the job. It was the worst new year they could ever remember.

* * *

Baglan Bay Refinery

Charles Meddison was seated in the main control centre of the Swansea refinery. There was no short-cut to working out why the catalytic cracking plant at the site had shut down at precisely five past twelve.

He had to work his way through six complex computer programmes in other sections of the refinery to check if anything had triggered the close-down of the plant. He also had to check that once it was restarted, nothing else in the system would be affected.

John Maples was seated behind him, cup of strong coffee in hand. He was fighting to keep awake. The shift manager was on the radio to the site teams and cross-checking the readings in the localised areas with the readings on the VDUs in the control room.

Meanwhile, in the distance, an emergency siren howled relentlessly. The cracking plant siren had been running for several hours, but there was no way to turn it off until the computer fault was rectified.

The closure of the plant was a major embarrassment. It produced 1.5 million tons of petrochemicals and plastics every year, as well as running an extensive gas separation system. Normally the plant never closed, and even on millennium night its 600 employees should have known nothing different apart from a 'millennium salmon or haggis special' served through the two large canteens and seventeen messrooms. As it had turned out, no one had eaten. They were all following a well co-ordinated drill which ensured that every aspect of the plant's processing equipment was fully monitored and reported.

No one had eaten, that is, except Jez Parker, who had consumed both a salmon and a haggis meal in the plant's emergency medical room. He was attended by two attractive young nurses who had cleaned his cuts and stitched his abrasions and kitted him out with a new set of underwear and overalls. It hadn't turned out to be such a bad millennium night for Jez after all. The worst thing about the whole experience was that his sodden lighter and cigarettes had been confiscated by security at the main gate. He couldn't remember the last time he'd been without a smoke for over three hours.

Things on the periphery of the plant in the cargo-loading area were much more normal. Already the first of the 350 tankers to be loaded for fuel delivery on new year's day were arriving to receive their cargo, and there was sufficient supply in the storage tanks to keep the system moving. The tanks contained 600,000 barrels of oil, and the floating roof on each gave an indication of how full they were. There was enough in the storage at Baglan Bay to supply the whole of southern Britain for three days, but the closure of the main refinery would cost the company more than 75,000 dollars an hour. Refineries are expensive pieces of plant designed to run all day every day.

Charles Meddison was still fighting to focus through his alcoholic haze. He had a thumping headache, and the nausea he'd felt earlier kept returning. It was hard to concentrate when you hadn't slept for over twenty hours and were trying to absorb half a bottle of prime whisky into your weary system.

He checked each programme to ensure that it had not been affected by the millennium bug, and was working on the catalytic cracking programme just as the general manager arrived at 3.50 am. He had driven from a family party in Middlewich the moment his pager had alerted him of the problem. He was not a passive man, and he stalked up and down the control room like a caged animal. He felt that Charles Meddison was being far too casual. He couldn't believe that after two-and-a-half hours of work, Charles hadn't yet got the problem sorted.

In the early days of the oil industry the separation of the main factions by distillation was all that was required. But to meet the demands for premium-grade oils and other advanced products, the oil had to be subjected to a process which would change its molecular structure by means of a chemical reaction. The catalytic plant reduced the larger heavy molecules into smaller, lighter and more valuable oil and gas molecules.

The catalyst used at Baglan Bay was ulimina-silica, it was powderheated and fluidised to pass between the reactor and the regenerator sections of the unit. There were over 150 tons of catalyst in continuous circulation at Baglan Bay.

With the computer systems checked, all that remained was to reboot the Honeywell computer controlling the cat-cracker. A team of engineers was positioned in the localised control room, and the site management team was standing anxiously behind Charles Meddison. They were watching his every move.

'Well, one thing's for sure,' Charles muttered, 'you ain't got no millennium bug here. You've got a computer failure in the control of the regenerator head.'

Figures whirred down the screen as Charles Meddison moved his hands deftly across the keyboard. Once it was rebooted the team at the sub-control unit cross-checked the figures from their readings.

'Time to party.' Charles Meddison smiled. He had done everything by the book, and everything looked fine.

139

Charles felt a surge of relief that this complex operation was over. He had done everything he should have done, everything that was, except compensate for the fact that Bemer's Vertex 2000 programme makes computers run twenty per cent slower than usual. When the computer controlling the catalytic cracker lost that much speed it no longer fed the ulimina silica from the reactor to the regenerator at precisely the right time.

'Cross-check complete. Reactivation begins.'

For some moments everything appeared normal. The screens flashed 'OK'.'OK'. 'OK'. No one in the control room noticed that the pressure in the catalytic unit was building. Slowly and silently a vacuum was being formed. Suddenly, somewhere, in the distance, Charles Meddison heard a rumble. And then all hell broke loose. It was 4.10 am.

Jez stood in the doorway of the Baglan Bay Refinery medical unit and gazed up at the giant plume of orange flame and white smoke which was pouring out of the cracking unit high into the darkness above.

In the far distance he could already see the Refinery's three fire engines racing to the scene. Within minutes two of them were drenching the area around the catalytic unit with thousands of gallons of sea water drawn directly from the harbour while the third was drenching the main tower with plumes of pure white foam.

Every possible emergency is rehearsed and planned for in an oil refinery. Even during Charles Meddison's doomed computer operation, the six employees and their ganger foreman at the cracking unit were giving readings from a specially constructed fireproof bunker. Elsewhere on the site all those employees not directly involved with the incident had been evacuated to a safe distance.

As he stood and watched, Jez marvelled at the great

inferno raging in the sky. It reminded him of paintings by Dante, an artist whom he had long admired, and had often sought to emulate in his own depictions of the supernatural.

Ten minutes later the Refinery ambulance returned to the medical unit with three casualties. One was a minor burn caused by falling ash which had landed on the face of a worker in the vacuum distillation unit on Lower Refinery Street, another was a lady from the canteen who had scalded her hand on the steam from a coffee machine as she rushed to complete her evacuation procedure . . . and finally there was Charles Meddison.

The ambulance driver reversed the vehicle to the main entrance and as they had rehearsed in their triage exercises the nurses labelled Charles with a large number '1', Number 2 was the burn, and 3 the scalded hand.

Jez moved into the surgery to watch them. They worked quickly and efficiently yet with great sensitivity. They were checking Charles's vital signs. In a matter of minutes a whole squadron of ambulances, police cars and fire engines from Swansea and Port Talbot would be on the scene. But in emergencies like this every second counts.

Minutes later the younger of the two nurses started to giggle. Partly it was a release of tension from the previous quarter of an hour, but partly it was because she just found it so funny.

'What's wrong?' the older nurse looked across, still checking the heart monitor.

'Smell his breath.'

The senior nurse leant forward and smelt. 'He smells like a blooming brewery.'

They continued working through the prescribed list of tests, but as each reading came back normal, the more relaxed they became. In triage exercises at the plant they'd never had to prioritise a drunk.

141

Little did they realise, however, that the blood sample they were taking was the most important blood sample which Charles Meddison would ever give. It was the sample which would end his career in the oil industry. Global Oil and its partners had a universal agreement with all of their employees that any sample registering above fifty per cent of the legal drink-driving limit led to instant dismissal.

Meanwhile, back in the control centre the general manager and the shift manager were locked in deep conversation with John Maples.

'Who the hell do you think you are telling me how to run my plant?' stormed the general manager.

'I am head of Scenario Planning, and tonight I carry the authority of the CEO of Global Oil and all its partners.'

'I don't want the press here. I don't need the press here. We've got enough problems in this place without inviting every reporter in the country to come snooping around.'

John Maples straightened himself. He was nearly a foot taller than the general manager. 'I don't care what you want or don't want, I am calling a major press conference and it will be held in the main tech-ops room at 9 am. I am going to explain what happened in words of one syllable, and you are going to back me up every inch of the way.'

He stared down at the general manager. He didn't need to say more.

'And what are you going to tell the press?'

'That the catalytic converter developed a rare fault and that we have already discovered how to ensure that it will never happen again.'

'That's total whitewash.'

John Maples smiled. 'That's what I'm paid for. Whitewash. And it's cheaper by the gallon.'

142

Over at the medical unit Charles Meddison opened a bloodshot eye and looked up at the ceiling that was swimming above him.

'Happy new year, nurse.'

She smiled back at him. 'Looks like you've been celebrating all night.'

Charles Meddison hadn't been at a party, he'd been at a wake. He was in mourning for a dead marriage, a lost family, a ruined life. Somehow he felt that over recent months he'd become disconnected from reality. He'd given his life for a fantasy. He bitterly resented Global Oil Networks and all it stood for.

The nurses completed their range of tests and moved on to prepare the other two patients for their transfer to Swansea General Hospital. There was nothing they could do for Charles Meddison except allow him to sleep it off.

Jez meandered over to Charles Meddison's stretcher and looked down at him. 'Aren't you the guy that gave me a lift on the Gower?'

Charles smiled weakly. 'Yes, I suppose I am.'

'I owe you, mate. Thanks a million.'

'Where are you going, I mean, now you've finished your job here. Back to the airport?'

It was a good question. Where would he go from here? Back to Houston? Back to London? Back to the airport? The possibilities floated past him, each one totally inappropriate. In that moment his greatest nightmare wasn't the loss of his job or admitting the disastrous mistakes he'd made in the control room. His nightmare would be meeting the general manager again, and facing up to the conflict that would follow. Charles Meddison couldn't face conflict no matter where he found it.

Jez repeated the question because Charles seemed miles away. 'Where are you going?'

'I don't know,' Charles sighed drunkenly. 'I don't know where to go. Got any ideas?'

'You can come back with me if you like.' Jez smiled warmly.

'Thanks. Where do you live?'

'On the Gower. The most beautiful place in Britain. You should see it. Spectacular it is. And great for surfing. Do you like surfing?'

Charles smiled. Yes, he did like surfing. He'd spent the last four summers at Fort Walton surfing in the Gulf of Mexico with Susan. He loved the sense of freedom it gave. 'Yep. Good surf is it?'

'It's brilliant. Bit cold, mind. You need a wet-suit. But I can get you kitted out no problem.'

'Live with your folks, do you?' Charles asked politely.

'No. I live with my mates, actually. We're into ecology.'

'What, recycling and all that stuff?' Charles had lots of unhelpful images of eco freaks.

'No, not really. We're into Mother Earth.'

'So what does that mean?' Charles was interested.

'We believe that the Earth is a living being, with subtle force fields. She is pregnant with every kind of embryo. She is the bountiful source of all fertility.'

'Not very scientific, is it?' Charles couldn't credit that in a scientific age such ideas still persisted.

'Precisely. The essentially feminine Earth was replaced by a machine in the scientific revolution. Today we are arriving at a new understanding of the world. We are beginning to regain mystical sympathy with the world.'

Charles Meddison looked confused. All this was news to someone who had devoted his life to electronic data interchanges. 'So what effect does it have on you?'

'We believe that we must learn to think wholeness, recognise the reality of the Earth Mother and see that our exploitation of the animal kingdom and the rest of nature is piling up for us an enormous karmic debt.' Jez was repeating verbatim what he'd heard from the others.

'And so you live simply?'

'Yes, but we live well. But come and see. You'll love it!' Jez relished the thought of introducing a new convert to the community. Especially someone from the oil industry.

Charles Meddison couldn't care less where he went, but he knew that he had to go somewhere. He certainly wasn't welcome at Baglan Bay Oil Refinery, or what was left of it. If nothing else, a few days surfing with Jez could be mildly entertaining and a good antidote to eighteen months of stress.

CHAPTER 5
Millennium Morning

The vicarage. Wandsworth

Helen Roberts tiptoed into the study with a freshly brewed cup of tea. The study was forbidden territory as far as she was concerned. James liked to keep that part of the house completely to himself. Early on in their marriage he had made it very clear that everything in the study had its proper place and that when anything was moved it distressed him. He was an orderly and precise kind of man.

As she pushed the door open she saw James slumped over his desk. He was in a deep sleep. She placed the cup on the desk beside him and placed her hand gently on his shoulder. She sensed his struggle, and silently prayed for him as she had done so many times down the years. Marriage was such a strange thing, but perhaps not quite as strange as cohabitation. Helen remembered her visit to Josh and Marie's tepee a few weeks before

* * *

'Married? Us? You must be joking!' Josh said convincingly. He and Marie were entertaining James and Helen to afternoon tea in the tepee. It was quite the strangest tea party which Helen had ever attended.

'Why not?' James asked. 'You're very much in love, aren't you?'

Marie poured him another cup of tea from a huge china teapot embossed with a Royal Coat of Arms and a picture of Prince Charles and Lady Diana. She'd bought it at the Rhosili Women's Institute Christmas sale.

'Just because we're in love, it doesn't mean that we want to spoil everything by getting married, does it?' Her Welsh lilt emphasised the 'does it?'

Josh poured four teaspoonfuls of sugar into his mug. 'The way we see it, we're committed to each other and that's all that counts.'

Helen smiled and sipped from the cracked mug she was holding. It was the strangest cup of tea she'd ever tasted, a kind of mixture of mint and dill. 'But shouldn't that commitment be made before God and enshrined in law?'

'Is your relationship better than ours because of that?' Josh asked pointedly.

Helen paused. It was a good question. Was their relationship better because they were married? There had been times over the years when their relationship hadn't been good at all. In fact, there had been times when it had been practically non-existent. The pressure of church duties had sometimes driven a wedge between them which had made them entirely separate and self-sufficient. Hardly a couple at all.

James came to the rescue. 'No, that doesn't make our relationship better. It just gives us a bit of extra help when we're struggling.'

'You don't struggle, do you? I thought that people like you had really got it together.' Josh took a deep swig of tea and put the mug down on the canvas floor.

Helen smiled. 'Yes, we struggle. We really struggle. Sometimes I don't know if we'll make it. The promises we made to God keep us going when we want to give up.'

'Perhaps you should stop struggling and just quit,'

Josh said sharply. He didn't believe in prolonging things that should be terminated.

Marie smiled at Helen sympathetically. There is a connection between women which men never fully understand. There was a pause and then Marie whispered, 'I struggle, too. I know what you mean. I struggle with the kids, and sometimes I struggle with you, Josh.'

Josh looked at her like a hurt child. He was speechless. He picked up the mug and downed the dregs of sugary syrup that lay at the bottom.

James tried to navigate the conversation into a lighter vein. 'Well, if ever you'd like a church wedding, I'd be happy to officiate.'

'Thanks for the offer, vicar, but I don't think that church is our kind of thing.'

Marie and Helen were looking at each other. They were both from South Wales, and they both shared a common heritage. Helen knew that, deep down, Marie wanted a white wedding, and that she wanted it in a church. She'd just never got round to telling Josh.

* * *

'Bad night, love?' Helen whispered. James stirred and lifted his head. 'Is it morning?'

'It's seven o'clock and the phone's been ringing on and off for the last twenty minutes. It's Radio Four, they want you to do an interview over the phone in about fifteen minutes. They're asking the Bishop, too.'

Helen sounded excited at the prospect of such an opportunity. James sat up. A shower of icy cold fear swept over him. Were they going to put him up against the Bishop? Surely they wouldn't do such a thing would they?

The phone rang and James Roberts, still struggling to greet the new day, reached out and pulled it to him.

'James?'

James knew that it was the Bishop. 'I'm very disappointed. The most wonderful opportunity of your career and you ruined it. What a mess.'

'Sir?' James was struggling for a reply. 'You mean the sermon?'

'Of course I mean the sermon. I've already had an ITN camera crew at my door and now it's Radio Four.' Radio Four was the station listened to by most of those in the church institution, it was always better to keep Radio Four away from church-based controversy.

'What's the problem?'

The Bishop nearly exploded. 'What's the problem? You're the problem, James. Pontificating on about disestablishing the church. It's none of your damn business. And using the pulpit at the Abbey to say it. The Dean phoned me at 2 am to tell me.'

'I'm sorry, Bishop, but I happen to believe it.' James hated confrontation, but, where necessary, he was ready to stand his ground. Helen stood beside him and gently massaged his neck. Whether he was right or wrong, she didn't really know, but she knew that he needed her now, perhaps more than ever.

'Well, James, the Dean and I are now in a very awkward position. The last thing we need is you blabbing your mouth off on millennium day. I forbid you to talk to anyone in the media. As far as we're concerned you're unavailable for comment. Just keep out of sight. Do you understand me, James?'

'Very well, Bishop.' James Roberts knew that if he didn't obey he would have to face the corporate wrath of the entire establishment. Bishops, like deans, were created to be obeyed.

Helen bent down and kissed him softly on the cheek. 'It'll be OK, love. Promise.'

It was one of those marital phrases that they had spoken to each other over and over again down the years when they were facing trouble. It resonated with memories and spoke with rich meaning. Somehow, it made him feel safe.

'The Bishop's ordered me to be silent. I'm gagged. If I say anything there'll be big trouble.'

'Then be silent, James. But don't just make it a silence without words, be silent within, too.'

He looked up at Helen's greying hair and freckled face and reached out to touch the gentle curl of hair behind her ear. She was older now, but in moments like this he loved her more than he had ever done. Perhaps they were getting through the struggle. He felt that, even if the whole world turned away, she would still be there. She understood. Now, more than ever.

She knelt down in front of him, and leant forward to kiss him. It was a kiss of warmth, of tenderness, of compassion.

'Helen,' he was looking intently into her eyes. 'Have I blown it, I mean, really blown it?'

She smiled. 'Probably James, but that's exactly why I married you. I enjoy living dangerously and . . . '

'And?' he was looking almost pleadingly.

'And I think that what you said in the sermon was right.'

He stood up and stretched. He ached in every bone in his body. He had been wrestling with his demons that millennium night and it had taken every ounce of his strength. If Helen thought that what he'd said was right, he could cope. Ultimately, he sought her approval more than that of the Bishop. Besides, the Bishop didn't make good apple pies.

* * *

Rhosili. The cottage

On millennium morning, following Matins, Anita Atwell was feasting on wheaten bread and home-made marmalade for breakfast. She didn't live a life of luxury but she did enjoy life's small pleasures. She didn't know how Maidoc had survived on his staple diet of barley and water out there on the Worm. She really appreciated her central heating, her freezer and her gas oven.

Perhaps she had deprivation enough. No car, no television, no supermarkets. She missed a lot of the things which she'd enjoyed in London. And, of course, she missed her walking. Such a simple pleasure she'd so little appreciated and now so sorely missed. In her own way Anita was as much a hermit as Maidoc. She was as cut off in her cottage as Maidoc had been cut off on the Worm.

Anita's pattern of daily discipline revolved around the daily disciplines of her Christian order: matins, the noon prayers, evensong and compline. She had started off as a novice in the Sisters of the Seashore, and Mother Superior had come to live with her for four weeks to 'get her started', as she had put it.

And so she had begun. Reciting the written prayers slowly and thoughtfully at first, pausing after each line for a moment's reflection. And then, as the familiar words had become a part of her, she had begun to add in extra prayers and readings and spaces for silent contemplation. Mother had taught her that to pray was to work, and that prayer demanded as much labour as digging a trench or building a wall. There were days when the work of prayer was heavy and demanding and days when it flowed with joyful ease. But prayer was Anita's work.

Anita needed to create a structure for her hermit life if it was to lead her to fulfilment. She needed to look back over every day, just as she did when she was a teacher, and savour the deep sense of accomplishment.

Anita's day wasn't all prayer and devotion, of course. On fine days she sat out on the veranda and read. When she was well enough she cooked. Sometimes she painted small water-colours of her spectacular views of the bay. And then there was her music. She loved Rachmaninov, whose powerful piano music gave her a foretaste of the rapture of eternity. She could never understand why Maidoc hated music.

Social contact was limited. She was disappointed that so many of the locals seemed reticent to visit her. She could only guess at what kind of reputation she must have gained. The villagers probably saw her as a poor spinster who was running away from reality.

The boy from the local grocery shop delivered whatever she ordered, and her pension was paid directly into the bank. She could manage quite well, but she lived with many disappointments. Her teaching friends from London had not remained friends for long. Within weeks of her move to the Gower they had stopped phoning, and her letters remained unanswered. They didn't really understand.

Perhaps, in the early days after Mother Superior had left her, her biggest struggle lay in the pressure of living alone. Completely alone. It hadn't mattered in London. There were always people around, and she was quite glad to retreat into the quietness of her flat at night to escape the madding crowd. But here it was different. Before Josh and his friends had arrived there had been weeks when she had hardly seen a soul. Maidoc had said that if you can know yourself, you can know God. Anita had found this challenge to be the hardest. Getting to know and to understand herself in those long dark nights of winter was very difficult.

Sometimes, however, her house rang with her laughter. A laughter which came bubbling up through her, triggered by some deep inexpressible joy which surpassed human understanding. Sometimes it came with a phone call from one of the other Sisters telling her about some funny incident. Sometimes it came with an unexpected letter. But mainly it came from the joy of watching the world just outside her veranda window.

The more she had read of Maidoc and the desert fathers the more intrigued she became about the connection they made between knowing God and knowing his created works. Slowly she began to make the same connection herself. Her binoculars brought a constantly changing feast of natural wonders into her living room. Above all, the beautiful birds of the Gower kept her enthralled at God's creative power.

In April she welcomed back the swallows and the house-martins, later she panned the rocky skyline with her binoculars to watch the first swifts as they arrived. She would gaze at the gorse bushes beneath her window where a nest of stonechats sometimes stood and watched her from their thorny perches.

On Worm's Head her binoculars clearly picked out the distant shapes of razorbills, guillemots and kittiwakes. Anita Atwell's veranda window was as good a hide as any bird-watcher could ever want. Day after day as she watched the whimbrels, the ring ouzels, the wrynecks and the occasional puffins and gannets she would wonder at the abundant generosity of her God.

Mother Superior had put it so beautifully. When someone knits you a jumper, paints you a picture or writes you a poem they express their love through what they have made. It was the same with God. His creation spoke of his generous love through every flower and cloud and changing season. He spoke through every shade and scent and texture. And all that he spoke was love.

So Anita Atwell's most treasured possession was not her ageing stereo, nor even her central heating, it was her binoculars. They rested on the coffee table beside her blue pot, and they gave her wings to fly free from her hermitage to explore the created wonders beyond. One day, before the last migrating birds had left the Gower in October, she had introduced Dave Rushden to the joy of ornithology.

* * *

'Look over there, in the tree, see?' She handed Dave the binoculars.

Dave peered through them and grunted in approval. He could see. He was enthralled. The more he knew about Mother Earth the more committed to ecology he became.

'Mother Earth is wonderful. She is the life-giver,' he said.

Sister Anita gently pulled the binoculars away from him. 'Mother Earth is not the life-giver, Dave. God is the life-giver, none other.' Sometimes there was a hardness in her voice, but only when things precious to her were threatened.

'I'm sorry. I didn't realise you felt so strongly.'

'David, if you imagine that the Earth is part of God, or even is God, you contradict his transcendence. His otherness from the world that he has created is what marks him out as transcendent. He is the one who has made all things, who alone stretched out the heavens and who created these birds we've been watching. If you think that the Earth produced it all, you are dangerously misled.'

'But surely we need to revert to an organismic world-view.'

'Sometimes, David, I despair of you. We don't need an organismic world-view, we need a new sense of God as the creator and sustainer of it all.'

She loved Dave and Josh, and Marie and Scott and Suse and Jez and the girls. She loved them all. But she ached for them to share her faith. She longed that they would not only see the spiritual world beyond, but the Christ who was, and is, and is to be.

* * *

Anita took another slice of wheaten bread and coated it with butter and chunky marmalade. The Rhosili Women's Institute made wonderful marmalade. It was a new millennium, and Anita Atwell felt glad to be alive. It had certainly been a remarkable few months. Perhaps God had heard her cries of loneliness. Perhaps he'd listened to her silent, tearless sobbing in the night. Perhaps he'd known her heart. Yet, of all the people to send to her obscure hermitage, why had he sent her New Age travellers? Perhaps he hadn't been able to persuade anyone else to come and share her seashore hermitage!

Best of all, God had sent her Jem and Pol, two of the liveliest children she'd ever met. After all those years with children she'd thought it would be paradise to be without the constant clamour for attention. How wrong she'd been. How, in her early months on the Gower she'd missed the excited squeals of play-time and the wide-eyed wonder of young minds making new discoveries. She'd mourned the loss of the innocent laughter which only children can bring. She'd discovered that a world without children was like a world without hope.

But God had brought Jem and Pol to her, and for the first time in her life Anita Atwell had understood what it was like to become a grandma. It had started in

155

October when Josh had knocked at her door and asked her another favour, the biggest favour yet.

* * *

'Anita. Thanks for having us, and thanks for giving us the space.' He always spoke quickly when he was asking a favour, as if he wanted the business over and done with. 'But the school man's been round and he says that if Jem's going to stay at the village school she'll just have to learn to read. I wondered if you could help.'

And so began the most rewarding teaching job Anita had ever undertaken. Only one child in the class, and only one subject — reading! What a privilege it had been, and what a joy! After Jem got back from school and had her tea she would run excitedly to Anita's door and announce, 'It's story-time grandma!'

Grandma Atwell and her solitary student Jem would sit at the window overlooking the Worm and share together the joy of stories and the wonder of books. Anita Atwell was running the happiest class she'd ever known. In the simple affection of her adopted grandchildren she found new hope, and discovered that God is no one's debtor.

* * *

The orchard

Josh didn't sleep for long. No matter how tired he was, he always got up early. He was a morning person and a day without morning was, as far as Josh was concerned, a day without a beginning. He especially didn't want to miss the first morning of the new millennium.

It was cold, and he lit a fire outside his tepee and

boiled water for coffee. He sat warming his hands for some minutes and then he took an old notebook from his anorak pocket and began to write.

* * *

It was 8.15 am and at last the senior nurse at Baglan Bay Refinery was ready to discharge Charles Meddison and let him go. He and Jez clambered into the taxi which John Maples had ordered for them. Maples saw Charles Meddison as an embarrassment. If the press discovered that one of Global Oil's top technical personnel had caused a major refinery explosion while under the influence of alcohol they'd have a field day. John Maples needed to get Charles out of the way before the reporters arrived. He knew how to handle the press. He would use simple words to explain the technical complexities of the process — and defuse the whole situation so that it didn't warrant many column inches. Charles Meddison could only complicate the process.

Charles and Jez sat in the back of the taxi as it sped along Upper Refinery Second Street, past the massive tankers in Lower Wharf First Street, and out towards the tall metal gates and the beckoning security man. Even as they passed the gates the first of the TV news units was approaching. Its roof scanner would carry John Maples' whitewash to the furthest points of the planet. Charles Meddison sighed as the taxi sped beyond the gates. He was now on the outside looking in.

The taxi meandered through the dockland streets of Swansea and along the road which follows the sweep of the bay and up the steep high street of Mumbles. Charles Meddison could barely keep his eyes open. His life had changed beyond all recognition in the few short hours since he'd last travelled down these unfamiliar roads.

* * *

Josh finished writing, downed the last of his coffee and crept into the tepee. Marie and the girls were still sound asleep. He placed the paper on the pillow, next to Marie's long dark swathe of hair, and crept out again. It was time to wash.

The taxi stopped outside the orchard gate and its two occupants climbed wearily out. Jez said that he would have paid if he could but, as he'd got no money on him, he couldn't. Charles smiled. He liked Jez, even though he couldn't begin to understand him.

Jez clanked open the orchard gate and they walked through the long damp grass. 'Is this it?' said Charles, feeling rather apprehensive.

Jez smiled. 'Yep, this is "Journey's End".' He pointed towards the rough wooden shack. 'And this is my place. Home sweet home.'

Charles wondered if he could get back to the road in time to stop the taxi, which was slowly manoeuvring in the narrow lane outside. It would take a ten-point turn.

'No, don't worry,' laughed Jez, 'you're not sleeping here, you'll be in the cottage.'

Josh was brewing another coffee over his open fire. He glanced across at the two figures by the wooden shack and leapt to his feet racing across the tall grass towards them.

'Jez . . . Jez . . . I thought you were dead!'

Jez laughed long and loud. 'Me . . . dead? No way, I've been at the biggest firework display in town, haven't I?'

Charles tried to smile. 'Pleased to meet you, I'm Charles Meddison of Global Oil Networks.' He paused. 'Late of Global Oil Networks . . . .'

'Great to meet you. What's been going down? We saw the flames,' Josh asked excitedly.

Charles smiled again. 'I blew up the refinery. Call it my small contribution to the demise of fossil fuels.'

'Anyone who can blow up an oil refinery is sure welcome here.' And he held out his hand in greeting.

'I reckon the Sister will put him up. Don't you?' Jez smiled knowingly.

Josh smiled again. 'I'll be very surprised if she doesn't. Come over to the cottage and we'll introduce you.'

Meanwhile, in the tepee, woken by the sound of distant laughter, Marie stirred and reached out for Josh. He wasn't there. She opened her eyes and saw a note on his pillow. Hauling herself up in the bed she took the note and read,

When you whisper in the darkness
I hear gentle waves on warm sand.

And when you stroke my hair
I feel the summer breeze on a warm day.

And when your arms close tight around me
I lie secure in the strength of your warm embrace.

And when you kiss my dry parched lips
I know my thirst is quenched by sparkling wine.

And when you smile at me
I soar towards the sun's warm rays
And there are butterflies
And fields of wheat
And summer flowers
And the warmth of love.

She smiled. They were moving towards a new level in their loving, an intimacy which made life worth while.

* * *

Anita Atwell had put the kettle on for Charles, Jez and Josh, and was sitting by the veranda window listening to Jez as he unfolded the story of his adventures. There was a lot of laughter — there always was when Jez was around. Anita liked Jez, but had never really known him. There was, she felt, an unreality about his brusque humour which masked much more.

She'd prayed for him, of course, but she'd never really reached him. Never connected. Never penetrated beyond his laughter to discover what dark secrets had made him turn to drugs and sex for comfort. Never shared his pain.

Josh was sitting on the stool warming himself by the fire. He was more pleased to see Jez than he'd ever imagined and was glad that he was safely home.

A few minutes later Anita escorted Charles Meddison to her beautiful little guest room. She wheeled herself ahead of him down the narrow passageway to the special room that was always prepared for unexpected guests. Maidoc had taught that whoever wished to stay with him could do so and would be offered the best that he could give. In the same tradition Anita Atwell would host this stranger and would offer Charles fresh Welsh cakes when he awoke.

'You are very welcome here, Charles,' she said, smiling up at him from her wheelchair.

'Thanks. I'm very tired.' He was more tired than he could ever remember.

'I'm sorry you've had a rough night.' She looked at

him with loving eyes. He felt her reaching out to him in empathy.

'I've had a rough year.'

'Well, Charles, I will pray for you. That things will all work out.'

Charles smiled disbelievingly. He thought of his marriage, his family, his job. Everything was in ruins. Nothing could ever be the same again.

'I'll not be staying long,' he said. 'I'll be moving on in the morning.'

It was Anita's turn to smile. She felt intuitively that he had come to stay for longer, much longer. In fact, through some mystery beyond her understanding she'd been expecting him. He was just another of the many pilgrims who the Lord was sending to 'Journey's End'.

Anita Atwell returned to the lounge and to Josh and Jez. She was pleased that she had a nice guest room. She couldn't have asked Charles Meddison to sleep in the corner of a cave as Maidoc would have done.

'OK,' Jez smiled as he turned to Josh, 'you've heard my story. What happened to you guys out on the Worm after I left?'

'We got cold, the fire went out, we went to a cave, we sheltered, we waited for the tide, we came back home.'

'That all?'

Josh leant over the roaring fire. 'We found a special cave, actually, not just any cave. It must have been a sanctuary or a church.'

Josh looked across at Anita, and their eyes connected. 'I think we found the place you're always talking about. I think we found Maidoc's hermitage.'

Anita burst into a loud gale of laughter. 'You're kidding me! You're kidding me!'

'It's got a Celtic cross and some sort of stone table and it faces east.'

'And is it on a balcony above the cliffs?'

'Yes . . . but . . . . '

'That's great news. I must tell the Sisters.'

'Wait.'

Anita looked across. His face did not share her joy.

'It was a dark place and we had a bad trip. It was as if all the powers of darkness gathered there.'

Anita was not laughing any more. She was leaning forward. Earnest. Attentive. Waiting. There was more.

'And when the trip was nearly over I thought I heard a human voice crying from deep within the cave, "In the name of Jesus Christ. Be gone. Be gone. Be gone." Could it have been Maidoc?'

Anita smiled again. 'So now I know for sure. You've found Maidoc's cave.'

Josh looked up at her, as if to question, but he didn't speak.

'That was Maidoc's job,' she said, 'to fight the demons and to claim the power of Christ. He did it for others and he did it for himself, but ultimately he did it for God.'

'I don't understand,' said Jez. 'What was this guy on?'

Anita looked across at Jez. 'That's just the point, Jez, he wasn't on anything; not drugs, not booze, not sex, not even movies or consumer durables. The only thing that Maidoc was on was reality.'

'Still sounds like a bad trip to me,' smirked Jez. But Josh was silent. Focused. His mind replaying the overwhelming emotions of those moments in the cave. He couldn't escape the feeling that he'd been running for far too long. Perhaps today, millennium day, was his day to face the reality which Maidoc had discovered.

Jez stood up. He'd had a long night and this was all too heavy for him to handle. 'Bed-time,' he muttered, and sauntered out. Suse was waiting for him beside his wooden hut. They often met when Scott was out.

After the cottage door had shut the conversation continued, but it was deeper and more serious. 'I thought that Jez was dead, you know,' Josh confided. The whole experience on the Worm had deeply disturbed him.

'And what did it make you think?' Anita asked, sensing that this was a special moment.

'About the transience of it all. Here today, gone tomorrow.' He was looking down at his feet, scared to look her in the face.

'And what about eternity?'

'I don't know. I just don't know.' He shook his head, and brushed his hand across his unshaven stubble.

'There is no reincarnation, Josh. Believe me.' She was unusually firm. At last he looked up at her as she spoke. 'Jesus taught resurrection and he vindicated his teaching by rising from the dead himself.'

'But aren't we all connected to the great cycle of life?' He was struggling to make sense of what he believed.

'I sincerely hope not. The integrity and unique personality of each of us is preserved at death. We must trust the grace of God to judge us personally and with perfect justice.'

'So I can't choose which situation to take on in a future life?'

'No, Josh. Jesus said, "I am the resurrection and the life; he who believes in me, though he die, yet shall he live, and whoever lives and believes in me shall never die."'

'But what about the endless turning of the wheel?'

'That's your problem, Josh, you have no sense of where you come from or where you're headed. You just keep on running. You're on a great treadmill going nowhere. You can have a destination. It's the kingdom of

163

heaven. And you reach it through forgiveness of sins not the shuffling of karma.'

Josh gazed into her eyes. Neither of them spoke. Why was it that whenever he was in her presence, he sensed a tranquillity, a holiness, an aura, the like of which he'd never known before?

'And what did I hear in the cave?' He was almost childlike in his questioning. He believed in the supernatural, but it was something else to experience it.

'You heard Maidoc the priest.'

'A ghost?'

'No. One of the spectators in the grandstand of faith who is still cheering us on.'

'I guess he just got carried away and shouted a bit too loud?'

Anita Atwell beamed. 'Yes, Josh. Maybe he did.'

'And what do I do next?' Josh sat in the ruins of his failed philosophy.

'You know, Joshua Lake. You know.'

* * *

The vicarage. Wandsworth

James Roberts sat down and drank a cup of strong freshly brewed filter coffee. The phone was ringing again. He felt torn, he really wanted to answer it. He wanted to speak to the media and to spread his message about the Celtic Christians as far and wide as he could.

Helen looked at him and somehow knew. 'I'll get that . . . and say you're unavailable for comment, OK?'

'OK,' he whispered into his coffee mug.

Minutes later Helen was calling from the study. 'James, I think you'd better take this.'

It was Anita Atwell, and she needed his help.

164

* * *

Anita had first met James in early October. She was constantly amazed at the way that people came into her life. She felt that God sent them. James Roberts had arrived, windswept and unexpected, while researching Celtic Christianity for his MA thesis. But she sensed that there was more. He was searching for reality and for God.

She had told him all that she knew of the lives of the Celtic saints. Meanwhile, James Roberts had sat on the little wooden stool, and chewed on his third successive Welsh cake.

'If you had to name just one characteristic of the desert fathers and only one, what would it be?'

Anita looked at the binoculars which were resting on the table beside her and smiled to herself. 'The place of nature in the Christian vision. The lives of the desert fathers have shown me that a holy person is at one again with restored creation, but in the right order, with humanity in control.'

'And did this follow through into the lives of the Welsh saints?' James was fascinated.

'Yes and no. In the Welsh lives we can see that nature herself actively co-operated with the reality of grace in the Christian saint.'

'I've lost you, unpack that if you can.'

'Well, although the Welsh saint did occasionally control animals, he or she also became a focus for a new life which touched the whole of creation.'

'So that's why David's horse wanted to take Aidan back to Ireland?' he said excitedly.

'And why the curlew swooped to save Bruno's book of sermons from the waves.'

He smiled. 'And why the stags spontaneously

offered their services as dray animals to Brynach, Illtud and Teilo.'

James Roberts reached out for a fourth Welsh cake, then stopped himself, thinking it somehow impolite.

'Go on, go on, they're there to be eaten.'

James smiled, and took a fourth. 'So do you think the Welsh saints have anything to say to the contemporary ecology movement?'

'As the conservation movement warns people of the obvious disasters inherent in such careless disregard of ecological checks and balances, yes. It really does come close to the feelings of the Celtic church.'

'So what would they have felt about the destruction of the earth for immediate gain, or the wholesale obliteration of the South American rainforests, or the destruction of food to maintain prices while famine ravages the globe?' James Roberts was preaching a sermon, as he was prone to do when he got carried away.

'They would have felt angry, and they would have warned of wrath to come. They took the injunction in the eleventh chapter of Deuteronomy in all seriousness, that those who love God will have plentiful crops and good pasture for their cattle. Loving God implied loving what he had created, too.'

James had grasped it. 'So in practical terms love for God is shown by a proper care for the earth.'

Anita Atwell smiled again. 'Are you sure I can't tempt you to that last Welsh cake? You might as well finish!'

James looked at the remaining cake on the plate and resisted. He was determined to take control of his expanding waistline.

'To put it simply James, the Celts felt strongly that adherence to the will of God could be equated to responding to the rhythms and harmonies of the natural environment. If they flouted them, then disaster would surely follow.'

That day, during that first interview, a bond had been forged between them. James Roberts was fascinated by Anita's grasp of early Celtic Christianity, but there was more, much more. She exuded a peace and a kind of connection with nature which resonated with the lives of the saints that he was studying.

In all, James Roberts visited her ten times. His many hours of research in the dusty back room of the University library in Swansea over the previous two years were brought vividly to life in just two months. They were brought to life by someone who not only understood the Celtic Christians but who lived their faith from day to passing day.

Without really understanding it James Roberts had begun to travel a journey with Anita Atwell and the members of Josh's Rhosili community. It had started off with an academic interest in the forefathers of the faith, and it had ended with him kneeling in front of Anita's wheelchair and repeating after her one of the prayers of the early Celtic church.

The gift I ask, may it not be denied me,
Is peace between myself and God.
May I find the way to the gate of glory,
May I not be sad, O Christ, in your court.

In that moment he found the infusion of Christ in all things. He had reached his journey's end and had made his new start.

* * *

James lifted the receiver to his ear. 'Anita. It's lovely to hear from you. Happy new millennium!'

There was no greeting in reply because Anita was in a hurry. 'It's Dave, Dave Rushden . . . the young chap with that mane of dark hair . . . into ecology, remember?'

'Yes, of course. What can I do?'

'The police just phoned to say he's in St Thomas's, and he's lost his memory.'

'I'm on my way, Anita.'

She interrupted. 'But that's not all, he's under arrest for public-order offences involving the Prime Minister.'

James smiled. 'I always thought he'd go a long way, our Dave. Don't worry. I'll get it sorted.'

CHAPTER 6
Millennium Noon

St Thomas's Hospital. London

Dr Jane Jennings at St Thomas's was tired, but she was also angry. Of all the blur of faces which had passed before her during the long night of a new millennium one image did not dim — a patient writhing in distress while handcuffed to a trolley. That patient's welfare was her domain. It was unforgivable that someone with retrograde amnesia had been manacled like some wild animal while on her ward. At 8 am she phoned the duty commander at Scotland Yard and reminded him of the seriousness with which the medical profession viewed such incidents.

Jane vaguely alluded to the £20,000 compensation payment made to a woman prisoner for being restrained before childbirth. She also wanted a full explanation as to why the patient had been moved following his fall, details of which had been passed on to her by the paramedic who had attended the incident. Such an action could well have killed her patient. She assured the commander that all the relevant information was prominently attached to his case notes.

Things move quickly at Scotland Yard when there is a sniff of litigation. Within thirty minutes the commander had called back and indicated that they would not be pressing charges in lieu of the patient's condition and their current pressure of work. Unbeknown to Jane

Jennings some invisible transaction had taken place at the highest level of police management. It would never find its way into the paperwork relating to events on millennium eve in Downing Street.

James Roberts arrived at the Accident and Emergency Department of St Thomas's just before noon. He was surprised that Dave Rushden was still on a trolley, and still in his blood-stained denim shirt and jeans some twelve hours after being admitted. It had evidently been a busy night at St Thomas's.

'Dave, it's great to see you. How are you?'

Dave Rushden looked puzzled. 'Do I know you?'

James stopped. It was a chilling experience to look into eyes that you knew well but to see no hint of recognition. How could Dave have forgotten the hours they had spent together talking theology in his old army tent? And why didn't he recognise the man with whom he'd shared that memorable walk up Rhosili Hill?

* * *

James and Dave had walked up the hill one crisp clear October day. It was James's last day with the community before returning to London. They strolled through Rhosili village and up the steep path to Rhosili Hill, over six hundred feet above sea level.

Dave was forging on ahead. 'Come on, even an old vicar like you can manage this.'

James was panting. 'Less of the old!'

'Fantastic place this,' Dave continued excitedly. 'It's the highest point on the Gower.'

'What are the stones for?' James picked up a pebble and dropped it in his pocket, he often collected souvenirs on his travels.

'For hundreds of years every villager that climbed

this hill brought up a pebble and added it to the pile. Thousands and thousands of stones — so many, in fact, that builders have taken lots of them down again. The chapel at Pitton was built from them.'

'And the big piles of stones. What are they?'

'Signs of burial, the megalithic tombs are just down the bottom. This hill's been used for burial for generations.'

They stood on the top of Rhosili Hill and looked down over the village to Worm's Head beyond. They could see Somerset, Pembrokeshire, Carmarthenshire and far out to sea the distant shape of Lundy Island. It was one of those days when you could see for ever.

'I want to be connected to all this,' Dave was turning slowly round, as if to somehow capture the panoramic view on every side of him.

'And how can you do that?' James was fascinated. He'd only read about this concept of connection to all things; he'd never experienced it.

'Your Christian God is aloof, uninvolved in creation, and your religion is distant from the natural world.'

'So you think my God created the natural world simply to abandon it?' James frowned.

'There's a division between sacred and secular, you've got it in compartments. You can't see it as a whole. You can't hack the wonder of it.'

James began to turn around in time with Dave. It looked bizarre, as two grown men twisted slowly round. 'You couldn't be more wrong. My God inspires all, quickens all, dominates all, sustains all. That's what the Celtic fathers taught.'

'But your Christian culture can't grasp interdependence, and it doesn't respect nature or recognise our stewardship of the planet. You just can't hack it.'

James placed his arm on Dave's elbow to stop him turning. He grasped it tight and David winced.

'That's just it, David. I have grasped it. I do know it.' Suddenly James sounded urgent. Emotional. 'And it dominates my every waking thought. I just belong to an institution which doesn't understand, and it really hurts.'

Dave had stopped turning. The friendly banter was over. He had touched a nerve. As Dave looked at him he could see the pain in James's eyes. There was an intensity of silence, then James continued.

'That's why I came, that's what I was looking for. That underlying unity. And that's what I have found. Through Anita, and you, and Jesus Christ.'

Dave reached forward and clasped James's arm tight. 'And that's what you're scared you'll lose when you get back to London, isn't it?'

James paused and looked out to sea. Slowly and reverently he spoke familiar words.

> I bind myself today to the virtue of heaven,
> In light of sun,
> In brightness of snow,
> In splendour of fire,
> In speed of lightning,
> In swiftness of wind,
> In depth of sea,
> In stability of earth,
> In compactness of rock.

Dave Rushden looked at James intently, his black mane of hair blowing haphazardly in the wind. He respected him. They had travelled a journey together and there on Rhosili Hill they had found a place of common ground. God was all, and was in all.

Jane Jennings was looking at her clipboard as she sauntered into the room. 'Good morning,' she said in a tired
voice. She was near the end of a sixteen-hour shift. 'Do
you know this young man, Vicar?'

'Yes. He's Dave Rushden from near Swansea.'

She looked at Dave with affection. It amazed her
that sometimes you shared deep experiences with a
patient, experiences which would always remain a mystery. She wondered what they had shared.

'Well, Dave Rushden from Swansea. I've got some
very good news for you, the consultant neurologist has
seen your scan, and he's given you the clear from anything
serious. Basically, with a few weeks of tender loving care
you'll find that things are starting to come back to you.'

Dave Rushden looked at James Roberts and saw in
his sparkling grey eyes a great warmth and humanity.
Instinctively, he knew that here was a fellow traveller who
could be trusted. An older man who could be a father to
him. James didn't speak, but his look of compassion said
it all.

James turned to the doctor. 'Don't worry, I'll take
good care of him.'

* * *

The cottage. Rhosili

There are dark nights in every person's life, but the few
hours which Charles Meddison spent in Anita's cottage
were darker than he'd ever dreamed possible. He lay on
the bed but sleep evaded him. He didn't even move. He
just lay, motionless, in a depth of dark despair from
which there seemed no escape.

Charles didn't believe in demons, but he met his demons that morning. For, in the quiet stillness of Anita's cottage he came face to face with the emotions and fears that he had been suppressing for so long. He had been running for far too long but now there was nowhere to run. His past had finally overtaken him.

There, in the stillness, Beth and Jenni were shouting, 'Daddy', their faces stained with tears, their eyes wild and desolate. The vision came again and again, and with each shriek of anguish another wave of pain swept over him. As the children raced towards him he turned his back and ran. But as he ran they somehow overtook him and raced towards him again, shouting, 'Daddy . . . Daddy.'

There were other images, too. Images of the CEO saying, 'Every confidence . . . every confidence.' The distant rumble of an explosion. The acrid smell of burning oil. John Maples smiling confidently in a graveyard. He could hear himself groaning. A desperate plea for reassurance. Its constancy was somehow comforting. He'd lost his wife, his kids, his job, his responsibilities. He felt like hell.

Charles Meddison came to and wondered where he was. Perhaps he had dozed after all. The back-door of the cottage banged shut. His head throbbed with pain. Light was seeping round the sides of the curtains. He pulled the pillow over his head. At last Charles struggled out of bed and pulled on his clothes. He felt dreadful. His whole body ached, and his head throbbed from the night before. He pulled back the curtains and blinked as his eyes grew accustomed to the bright sunlight of midday.

He stared out at the view. It was spectacular. His window overlooked the bay and the blue sea stretched out to infinity. The strange shape of the Worm framed the left of the bay. The gulls were wheeling overhead. It was all very beautiful but he was too miserable to notice. He swilled his face in the sink beside the window and cupped his hands to drink of the fresh sweet water from the tap.

Charles slipped into his shoes, and stumbled out into the lounge. The cottage was deserted. Whatever this place was, and whoever these people were, it wasn't right for him. Charles Meddison straightened his back and walked through the empty orchard towards the road. The light was blinding him and his head throbbed. He knew exactly where he was going and precisely what he was going to do.

He scrambled over the grassy field, past the sheep which grazed so peacefully, and headed out towards the Worm. He was almost running and he was breathless. The tide was on the ebb, and the rocky ridge was freshly washed and revealed again for a few brief hours. Charles lunged forward onto the ridge, the sea water splashing upwards as he ran, his trousers quickly soaked, he tripped and fell, but dragged himself up again. He was driven forward by the scenes of his past and by an overwhelming force of self-destruction.

* * *

'Where will you go?' Susan had asked as she stood on the patio in front of the door to their Houston timber bungalow.

'To the Holiday Inn. You can call me there.'

'OK', she said, and turned back towards the house.

'And Sue?' he called. 'Take care of the girls.'

'I think it's a little late for you to be concerned for them,' she muttered, and closed the front door firmly behind her.

And so had ended a four-year relationship and a three-year marriage. As he drove out of the beautiful estate on the outskirts of Houston he wondered if he'd ever return. He feared he wouldn't. It was over. Finished.

Charles Meddison had never been very good at relationships. He could woo women, he could build relationships, he was a good lover, but he'd never been able to handle conflict. There was something deep within him which ran from it every time. Other men might have turned the car round, bought flowers, camped on the doorstep all night, done anything to start again with Susan. But not Charles Meddison. When things went wrong he ran. He always ran.

Charles Meddison's inability to resolve conflict was the real source of his marital difficulties. The demands of Global Oil Networks and the millennium bug were only the trigger. Even as he drove away, Susan Meddison was lying on the sofa sobbing, hoping against hope that he might return.

If he'd only said sorry, shown some flicker of remorse or offered to try again she would have opened her arms to him there and then. But as it was he seemed cold and heartless. It was no way to treat a woman.

Perhaps if he'd been a different kind of man he wouldn't have let the CEO of Global Oil bully him the way that he had done. But he just hadn't been able to face the possibility of conflict with his boss. He would rather work himself into the ground and dump on his family than call the chief executive and tell him that what he was asking was impossible.

That was Charles Meddison's problem, he couldn't face conflict. He couldn't look people in the eye and tell them how he felt. He couldn't say sorry. He couldn't say no. Charles Meddison preferred to run away. Chicken. Deserter. Defector. Traitor. Coward. Perhaps he was no man at all. And now the time had arrived for him to run from everything.

* * *

On and on he went, over Middle Worm and down the grassy bank to the ledge. He stood and looked down the two-hundred-foot drop to the surf-splashed rocks below. He was dizzy with the adrenalin of it. The man of decision had decided. Driven by demons of failure, of despair, of fear. Slowly he edged forward, and the faces of his children looked up at him from the surf below. 'Daddy . . . Daddy.' Their arms were open and they were calling him forward.

Silently, Scott strode out from Maidoc's cave and gripped his arm. He gripped it with such a force that Charles shuddered with pain. 'Who the hell?'

Scott's eyes blazed with anger. 'You have no right, not here.'

Charles shivered with fear. His children were below, some wild man above, he was trapped. He looked into Scott's eyes, half pleading.

'The duty of love,' Scott said.

Charles looked at him, not understanding.

'The law of love. The law of Christ.'

Charles was very, very scared. A kind of holy fear. An awe. A sense of being in the presence of something greater than himself. The coarse voice was urgent. Unbending. Demanding.

'I bind myself today to God's virtue to pilot me, . . . say it . . . say it.'

Charles felt the grip around his arm tighten. Slowly, and in the cold grip of fear, he spoke, 'I bind myself today to God's virtue to pilot me.'

Scott continued, phrase by phrase, waiting until Charles had echoed the words.

'God's might to uphold me, God's wisdom to guide me, God's eye to look before me, God's ear to hear me, God's word to speak for me.'

Charles' voice had tapered off into a whisper. Scott shook his arm again. 'Say it . . . say it.'

'God's way to lie before me, God's shield to protect me, God's host to secure me, against snares of demons, against seductions of vices, against lusts of nature, against every one who wishes ill to me, afar and near, alone . . . and in a multitude.'

Charles Meddison collapsed on the ledge into unconsciousness. He fell into a deep and healing sleep. For years to come he would relive those moments on the dark edge of human experience. For years to come he would thank God that Scott was standing in Maidoc's cave that millennium day and was ready to save him.

Charles Meddison had come back from the brink.

* * *

The church. Rhosili

Josh pushed Anita Atwell's wheelchair gently back up the central nave of Rhosili church. It was the millennium day treat that he'd promised her. Josh always kept his promises.

She'd paused to pray alone, before the altar, and now they were heading out into the graveyard to hear the special millennium peal of bells at midday.

Josh lingered by the font to look at the fourteenth-century bell inscribed, *'Sancte Tellaut ora pro nobis.'* It had been tolled by unknown priests in distant generations as they called their people to prayer. Next, he stopped the wheelchair by the north wall of the nave to stare at the pure white memorial tablet dedicated to a Rhosili man, Petty Officer Edgar Evans RN, who died in 1912 with Captain Scott on the tragic journey back from the South Pole. It bore the simple inscription, 'To seek, to strive, to find and not to yield.'

On they went, through the fine twelfth-century doorway of Rhosili church which was ornate with chevron and dog-tooth mouldings and with its battered carved heads as label stops.

'Eight hundred years this has been here,' Anita said, looking up at the doorway. Josh instinctively did the same. 'See, there's a scratch dial on it, once used for telling the time.'

'Amazing.' Josh loved this sense of continuity with the past. Some sort of permanence in a transient world.

'That's not all,' she continued, 'they believe this doorway was brought from a former besanded church on the Warren between the beach and the foot of Rhosili Downs.'

Josh pushed the wheelchair up the gravel path between the lines of gravestones and Anita pointed towards the large hewn stone on which was carved a Celtic cross. He pushed her towards it.

And then the bells began to peal, uncertain at first, but slowly building in intensity. Three in all, cast by J.Warner of London in 1893. Josh looked up at the tower with its saddleback roof as the waves of sound swept over them.

Anita struggled painfully from her chair and hobbled uncertainly towards the stone. She leant against it and closed her eyes. She smiled a broad smile. Here, on millennium day, she felt again that sense of connection with her forefathers in the faith.

A few minutes later came the soft peal of the bells of Llandewi drifting over the meadows on the gentle breeze. Anita pictured those early Christians from Gaul who had spread the gospel in Llandewi before the Roman military garrisons left at the beginning of the fifth century.

And there, in the distance, she could hear the steady toll of the church at Llangennith, and she remembered the squabbling fifth-century kingdoms and their godly leader Dewi, a Llangennith man.

Then came the sweet bells of Llanmadoc, the church dedicated to Maidoc, her hero. He'd been influenced by Patrick, and after his four long years of prayer on the Worm had gathered a congregation of hungry souls to found Llanmadoc church. The Llanmadoc bells were rising and falling up and down the scale. She pictured the little church, and remembered her visit there on Maidoc's feast day. Those bells were a celebration of all that she had gained from him.

The celebration was nearly over. Raggedly, the bells slowed and lost their power, yet still, in the far distance, the peal from Llanrhidian rolled gently onwards towards the sea, until at last it too was silent.

'Thank you, Josh. That was very special.' Anita struggled back towards her chair and slumped into it. Every joint in her body ached relentlessly.

'No problem.' Josh smiled as he pushed the chair through the churchyard gate. He had found a new sense of connection to the past.

'Josh,' Anita turned back and looked up into his face. 'Do you believe that history repeats itself?'

Josh looked puzzled. 'Repeats itself?'

He continued to push her, down the narrow road and in through the squeaking gate to 'Journey's End'. Suse was sitting on the single chair in Jez's make-shift cabin, and he was sitting cross-legged before her. They were deep in conversation. Scott was off on one of his long walks to the Worm.

Anita and Josh carried on, past the makeshift dwellings and back into the cottage. Neither spoke, but in the strange relationship between one who pushes and one who is pushed they were together.

Once inside the cottage, with Anita seated beside

the veranda window, and Josh crouched on the stool
beside the embers of her fire, he made his first confession.
He confessed a life in search of escape. A life of unreality.
A life of running away.

Solemnly he knelt before Anita as she leant and
administered olive oil in the form of a Celtic cross on his
forehead. She prayed the most beautiful prayer that he
had ever heard:

> I bind myself today to the virtue of heaven,
> In light of sun,
> In brightness of snow,
> In splendour of fire,
> In speed of lightning,
> In swiftness of wind,
> In depth of sea,
> In stability of earth,
> In compactness of rock.
>
> I bind myself today to God's virtue to pilot me,
> God's might to uphold me,
> God's wisdom to guide me,
> God's eye to look before me,
> God's ear to hear me,
> God's word to speak for me,
> God's way to lie before me,
> God's shield to protect me,
> God's host to secure me,
> Against snares of demons,
> Against seductions of vices,
> Against lusts of nature,
> Against every one who wishes ill to me,
> Afar and near,
> Alone . . . and in a multitude.

Although he didn't really understand it, Josh had planted his feet on a different path. There had been two paths ahead of him, and he had chosen the harder.

EPILOGUE

Maidoc's cave. 1 May AD 500. 12 noon

Maidoc looked up at the sky. A distant ridge of white cloud was retreating across the mainland, and the edges of it bore the orange reflections of the sun. It would be a warm and cloudless afternoon. Maidoc loved summer on the Worm, and on clear bright days like this he felt the pleasure of God in his creation.

As soon as he walked out of the cave and climbed the grassy embankment the gulls were wheeling overhead, calling to each other in excited cries of delight. They swooped and climbed, making ornate patterns in the sky. Through some invisible force he was part of them, and they of him. This wonder of the natural world did not come from some theological proposition, nor some ecological thesis. It came from a constant sense of connectedness to it all, the cycles of the seasons and the creatures that shared his island refuge.

Maidoc scrambled down the rough path towards the beach on the east of the island. The fresh air filled his lungs and the gentle breeze covered his face with salty moisture. It was time to search for soft crab. In the distance was the resonant hiss and boom of the blow-hole. The tide was on the ebb again. He knew that as the water receded from the high pools on the east of Middle Worm he would find a plentiful supply of edible crab. He scrambled over the rocks and found a large pool full of swirling

seaweed as ripples of seawater drained over the side and
followed the tide out to sea.

He ran his hand through the long green dulse and
scooped out his prey. He pulled out a hand-sized shell
with a pie-crust edge and a beige-pink back. Its black-
tipped nippers clawed at his gentle fingers. He placed it in
his brightly coloured shoulder bag, and then plunged in
his hand for a second one. This time the crab had drawn
itself up tall, and had wedged its back up against the
rocky ledge, and he had to prise it loose.

Next came the hunt for the whelks which were
spread out all along the rocky outcrop. The off-white
sculptured shells with their pointed spires were plentiful.
Just beside them there were mussels. He would soon have
a meal fit for a king.

As Maidoc climbed back up the steep path towards
his hermit balcony he recited the familiar words of the
prayer of praise he loved:

May plain and hillside praise you,
May the three springs praise you,
Two higher than the wind and one above the earth,
May darkness and light praise you,
The cedar and the sweet fruit-tree.
Abraham praised you, the founder of faith,
May life everlasting praise you,
May the birds and the bees praise you,
May the regrowth and the grass praise you . . .
And I too shall praise you, Lord of glory,
Hail to you, glorious Lord.

His lunch of shellfish over, Maidoc sat cross-legged and
looked out to sea. It was a beautiful day and the blue of
the sea and the blue of the sky met invisibly across the
horizon. It was hot, but the gentle breeze made it feel

very pleasant. Sometimes Maidoc was overwhelmed by the beauty of the Worm, and he felt glad to be alive. But even on days like this when the weather was fair and the spring flowers covered the grassy bank his life was tinged with sadness. For he was all alone and there was no one with whom to share the beauty.

Maidoc believed that all who found their way across the perilous tide and who wanted to meet with him deserved his best. No matter who they were or what they shared he always prayed for them. Some days no one came and he was left alone, exposed to the merciless howling of the wind and the damp spray of the restless sea. And at each ebb tide, as faithfully as the tolling of a church bell, his days were marked by the distant boom of the blow-hole.

Maidoc's long hours of focus on Christ had led him into a new sense of connection with the created order. He had stopped living in the past or the future and started to live in the eternal connection of each unfolding moment. He measured his disciplines of prayer by the rising and setting of the moon, and calculated the great festivals of the Christian year by the lengthening and shortening of the days.

His sense of at-oneness meant that he could sit motionless outside his cave for hours on end. The sea birds would gather round him to share the invisible connections of the created order. The rabbits would scurry past the opening to his cave without fear. The seals would bask in the long summer evenings in the caves below and cry out to him like children in search of a mother. He viewed the constant changes of weather as an unfolding declaration of the character of God. The winds spoke of his power and the warm sunny mornings of his renewing strength. The scudding mists of cloud told of his mystery and the buttercups which filled the grassy slope each spring spoke of his beauty and his love.

As the blow-hole marked the beginning of another ebb tide that warm spring day, he could hear some distant voices. There were strangers clambering across the damp ridge of rock newly washed by the tide. There were strangers clambering up Middle Worm and scrambling down the grassy bank. There were strangers from a different world and a different time. They had come to visit his holy place.

He could see them clearly now, clambering down the hill towards him. Each bringing with them their fears and nightmares, the brokenness of lives lived outside God's perfect plan. They were ordinary people. People haunted by the past and scared of the future. People trapped by demons within them and brought low by their weakness to resist.

Maidoc, the hermit of Worm's Head, had uncovered the great mystery of time. As he lived in the constancy of the ever-present moment he had discovered that time itself had disappeared. He lived in the immediacy of the living God, who was, and is and is to be. There, in this eternal presence, the past and the future compacted into now. Eternity was contracted to a span.

Yes, they were scrambling towards him now. This new generation long distant to his own. A people who had, for so very long, been separated from reality and confused by the fantasy of their civilisation.

He had wept for them. This godless, hurried people scurrying to make up time but missing the vast expanse of eternity. Grasping to possess but becoming possessed. Riding rough-shod over nature but missing the connectedness of all things. Making gods of themselves while God looked on. He had prayed that one day they, too, might have hopes and dreams. Hopes of a world beyond the transient business of their human plans. Dreams of a better life than money could buy.

They were coming towards the cave and he wanted to see them. He had been praying for them from his distant outpost. Praying that one day the territorial spirits of their age would be defeated and that, at last, they would be free.

First down the grassy slope came Jem, a beautiful woman now, tall and dark and assured; pausing half way to turn and help her younger sister down the bank. Pol was giggling as she always did. Life was so much fun when you were twelve and hadn't a care in the world.

Then came Josh, his hair longer now and his sideburns gone. He walked with a greater confidence. He was the long-established leader of a community recognised throughout the land as a place of prayer, of refuge and of the presence of Christ. On his back, slung in the security of a strong harness, was a young child pointing excitedly at the sea. Marie was by his side, she was talking softly to their son.

Charles Meddison ambled slowly to the steep drop of the cliff edge and looked down, as he had done so many years before. He saw the vision of his children Beth and Jenni again. But now they were smiling, and he was glad to be alive. Charles looked much the same, except for wisps of grey around his temple. Still in designer jeans, but his T-shirt now emblazoned with the logo of a new Christian movement called 'God's Earth' based in the community at Rhosili. The logo portrayed a globe with the faces of two children looking out with hope. He had found something else to live for and something else to die for. But this time his life wasn't given for a human corporation but was poured out for the kingdom of God.

Scott walked up beside him and placed a hand on his shoulder. No one ever knew what they had shared here so very long ago. They paused, each alone with their thoughts. Scott remembered the last time he had clambered down this slope with Suse. It had been a different time, a different life. But now she lived with Jez in Scotland. She was gone, but not forgotten. He had hoped she might have made the journey back today.

James and Helen Roberts came next. Him in his purple cassock, his face lined, his figure stooped, but his eyes still sparkling with the joy of life. Helen was by his side looking radiant. Happy. They had entered a new phase of life which had drawn them close.

Behind him, bringing up the rear, in suit and dog collar, came Dave Rushden, the newly inducted vicar of Rhosili. He was as tall and confident as ever. His hair was tied neatly back into a pony tail. Over his shoulder was slung a brightly coloured bag. As soon as he had negotiated the steep grassy bank he pulled the bag forward and took out a blue pot coated with wax. It was glazed with the sign of a yellow Celtic cross.

And everywhere there were butterflies. Small tortoiseshell, small coppers, peacocks, painted ladies and, most prolific of all, bold red admirals. They were fluttering daintily in the long grass and up and down the grassy slope. Hovering, almost motionless, in the tufts of hard straw along the cliff edge. The hiss and boom of the blowhole echoed down the cliffs. But today it tolled for Anita Atwell. James Roberts gathered his little flock around the entrance to the cave, facing seaward.

'Anita lived alone in a cottage near a cliff. Yet she affected our lives in ways that we will never fully understand. She prayed for us, and how she prayed! And, in praying, she came to love us with the love of Christ. We were all changed by knowing her. Our lives took different paths because of her. And so we come to this special place, a place she loved but never saw, to thank God for her and to scatter her earthly remains. She may be gone, but her prayers will last for ever.'

Josh nodded, and Pol took out a piece of purple writing paper and slowly unfolded it. She stood with her back to the cliff and addressed the little congregation. Her long dark hair was blowing restlessly in the gentle wind.

'This is a note from Anita, written just before she died. She asked me to read it to you on this day.'

All were silent, save for the distant squealing of the gulls. And as she began to read, Pol's voice quaked with emotion, for she remembered that without Anita she may never have read at all.

'My dear friends. Thank you for enriching my life. Thank you for loving me. Thank you for caring. As I prepared to leave you all I asked myself what are my hopes and dreams for the world? It's a question that has puzzled me ever since millennium night, but the more I thought, the more the answer seemed so plain.

You are my hopes and dreams. You. The people I loved and prayed for. You carry my hopes and dreams for the future of the world, but more than that, you are my hopes and dreams. For in your loving, your struggling and your praying you will help fulfil the greatest hope of all. Thy kingdom come, on earth, as it is in heaven.'

Dave Rushden took the blue pot and gently passed it to Josh. He stood, holding it out towards the horizon, tears streaming down his cheeks. 'I thank God for sending you to us, Anita, and now we release you back to Jesus.'

He gently lifted the lid and poured the fine white dust into the warm gentle breeze. Maidoc was close beside him, his gnarled hand reaching out as the dust of Anita's mortality raced through his fingers. He was looking up to heaven and smiling. The dust swirled above the cliff edge and dissipated, blowing out across the sea towards the horizon and on into eternity.

Maidoc started it, but soon the little group which was standing on the edge of the world were speaking it in unison.

> I bind myself today to the virtue of heaven,
> In light of sun,
> In brightness of snow,
> In splendour of fire,
> In speed of lightning,
> In swiftness of wind,
> In depth of sea,
> In stability of earth,
> In compactness of rock.

> I bind myself today to God's virtue to pilot me,
> God's might to uphold me,
> God's wisdom to guide me,
> God's eye to look before me,
> God's ear to hear me,
> God's word to speak for me,
> God's way to lie before me,
> God's shield to protect me,
> God's host to secure me,
> Against snares of demons,
> Against seductions of vices,
> Against lusts of nature,
> Against every one who wishes ill to me,
> Afar and near,
> Alone . . . and in a multitude.

Although he didn't really understand it, Maidoc knew that in the vastness of God's expansive love there is no time, nor space nor distance. Only communion with the one who is all, and is in all. The one whose purposes weave a tapestry across the generations. A tapestry whose intricate patterns are only seen or fully understood beyond the veil of knowing.